I0778140

The Holy Infant
or
AbaxaCataBax

Thomas Fox Parry

SPUYTEN DUYVIL
New York City

In June 2010, *The Holy Infant* by Józef Nowak found me. The book, a manuscript, was in the periodicals archive of the Philadelphia Free Library, Central Branch, sub-basement one. The pages had been divided between three envelopes and crammed into a banker's box otherwise full of moldering issues of *Der Philadelphia Burger*, a German-language newspaper that ran from 1876 to 1900. I was a temp, hired to digitize, and so I opened the first envelope, removed its pages, and laid the first sheet in my scanner. It read:

> *Dear Emil,*
> *Here is* The Holy Infant *as promised.*
> *Consider it.*
> *Need a subtitle? Try:*
> *The weird and thrilling narrative of a lost man.*
> *Alternate title:*
> AbaxaCataBax.
> *Yours,*
> *Józef*

As I digitized, I read, and eight hours later I emerged from that basement and onto the Benjamin Franklin Parkway. I stared at the traffic, the cathedral, the fountain and the skyscrapers. Nowak's *Holy Infant* was live in my thoughts. Many of the pages had deteriorated, turned to scraps with time, but I had read and digitized the survivors, and now an awful light escaped from the joints of the world. A sensation pierced my chest. I think I started crying. I'm still trying to get my head together.

I've added notes to *The Holy Infant*, just a few, to aid comprehension where the text was destroyed. I have also omitted the comments of Emil Zörner, to whom Nowak addressed the manuscript. Zörner was *Der Burger*'s editor and publisher. He was also a friend to Nowak. At turns, Zörner scribbled "Nonsense!" "Wise!" "God forgive you," and "Ahh …" in the margins.

Nowak had written *The Holy Infant* in English in hopes of broad readership, but in the end, Zörner counseled against carrying on with the project.

"Forgive me," he wrote to Nowak, "I fail to see the treasure here."

I see the treasure of *The Holy Infant*.

I don't know whether it's a true story. I don't know how much of it can be true. But then impossible occurrences cling to us. They lurk and intrude, stretch thought, run our feedback through new channels. Do you feel it?

The Holy Infant is an artifact of these forces. It's also, at minimum, even in its damaged form, the weird and thrilling narrative of a lost man, woman and child.

Nowak's manuscript has shaped my consciousness. It has obsessed me and changed my life. I am beyond grateful, and a little afraid, that it may do that for you.

Thomas Fox Parry
Philadelphia
2024

The Holy Infant
by Józef Nowak

[First Folio—Intact]

ONE

Klara was born in Hel, a fishing village at the end of a sandy spit that arcs into Danzig Bay. Despite the immensity of water around her, she grew up without any special feeling for God. She helped her father and punctured thousands of fish skulls with a nail through a wooden peg. The fish would stop thrashing. Their scales, tiny prismatic patches, would stick to her forearms, then dry, pale and fall away.

The sea once gave the village a crate of yellow bicycles. A boat of four fishermen once went out and never returned. One morning, Klara's mother gave birth to three dead baby girls. Klara's grandmother wrapped them in white, and they stayed in the house, side by side in a crib, and they stank. The third and smallest baby girl had no ears. The priest arrived and baptized them. Klara's father then buried them in the bay, which was not the custom.

Klara had two living sisters besides. Their mother, who was from Danzig city across the bay, taught the living girls to read. Klara enjoyed the journeys taken in the Bible and the ups-and-downs of its storybook Jews. Elves were only half-believed in by the grown-ups. Trolls not at all. Gnomes, yes. Dragons lived in the past. Water and wood spirits were real, and Klara had seen several of both.

Her mother, after the birth of the dead girls, bought a bell from the priest to keep evil spirits from their house. She rang the bell to call her daughters home for meals. Jesus was a carpenter and a fisherman, and so were his friends, and so was every man Klara knew. Except the priest. When he came to town, he carried on his horse Christ crucified on an anchor. Jesus lived on the seafloor with Klara's dead sisters, water spirits, and merpeople. At eight years old Klara wore a wreath of flowers and took First Communion and did not think of it as eating Jesus' flesh or drinking his blood, no matter how many times they said it. Mary, a virgin, gave birth. None of this ranked as strange in the Bible or in Hel. God and his people had adventures and demons spoke.

To Klara, ships were the mystery. Not boats, which were as normal as shoes and knives. But ships. Passenger ships and freighters. Ships sliding across the horizon without cease in all but the coldest months of the year. At times, distance layered up before them. But on a clear day, she could count the sails. Sometimes she could see the people. They were waving.

Klara's father was from Hel, but he had worked in the Danzig shipyards and had sailed as a ship's carpenter on a route to Lisbon and back. He was patient, had a strong memory of his adventures and explained to Klara from the bowsprit to the rudder how a ship moved across the water.

Yet ships belonged to another world, so said a strand that hummed within Klara.

The lighthouse understood. It stood up from the trees on the other side of the spit. At the top of its red brick tower, a limelight burned. Three times a day, its keeper fired a cannon.

One night when she was twelve, Klara awoke out of doors. She stood upon the flagstone with her back to the door of her family's home. It was summer, and the night held a cool thrill. Klara walked away from her home, Hel, the cluster of stone hovels, and went into the wooded rise that shielded the village from the wind of the Baltic. Klara climbed the rise, her feet on the soft bed of pine needles, and came to the stone at the peak, a broad rock that bristled with lichen in the moonlight. From a little further on, the infinite sea stretched. Along the beach waves broke, reaching down the spit with a curling hush. Klara headed for the beach, invited again by the night. She began a journey.

The night was unlike other nights, she thought.

The spirits had risen up in all things. From the hoods of the waves, spirits watched her, and they followed her, rushing through the tops of the trees. Their fingers touched between her toes through the cold of the sand. Their voices through the wind, the water, trees, brush and sand met her ear in a chorus, at once screaming and cooing. The spirits were in the salty break of the air on her tongue and the sting of windbourne sand on her legs. They moved in her blood and skin and at the roots of her hair. Before long, the beach ascended into a range of dunes, forming both a small desert and its temples. Klara climbed hand and foot to the tallest of the dune peaks and there she waited under the Moon.

The dunes had risen so high that they had covered part of the forest, and after a time, a wolf edged out from the half-buried trees. The wolf beheld Klara. More eyes were on her, more wolves standing amid the branches, and from the other end of the tree line came families of deer, shining stags, does and fawns. In the wall of tree tops, there were birds. They opened their wings to join the branches and leaves.

Klara then turned and faced the sea. At the foot of the dune, speckled seals wriggled from the surf, and further out, in large, black moves within the shimmering moonfield of water, whales appeared and disappeared. Klara felt fear, of course, but also felt another sensation.

She felt as though she were turning to vapor and stone at once. Time was both rushing and still.

Klara had been summoned there to witness, she was sure.

Out on the horizon was a ship. A black bar on the moon-brightened water. Its spars were bare, yet it moved. Black smoke rose from its center. The ship was on fire.

And all at once the night was over.

It was morning, just before dawn, and Klara was back in Hel. Gone were the dunes, the animals and the spirits, the Moon and the ship.

Klara was standing on the beach, but now only a short walk from the village. The cold sand had numbed her toes and heels. Boats were ashore on either side of her. It had rained in the night. Water in the keels reflected the sky. The smell of fish in the ropes and the wood was strong in the cold air. The horizon was dark sky and dark water, and from it, the bay reached toward her, rippling glossy and thick as it touched the sand. Klara was about to head home when a noise came from the trees.

The trees waved wet limbs. From the darkness

below burst forth the lighthouse keeper.

The lighthouse keeper was Adem Martens.

He was a foreign man in a blue coat. He had no hat. His hair was long and black and it flew up in the wind. On the sand, he fell to his knees.

"Young sister!" he cried. "What was that?"

Klara could not answer.

This was the first time a stranger had ever addressed her.

"The light!" he said. "What was it?"

She thought perhaps the man was speaking of his very own lighthouse, which was only a few dozen yards away, standing up from the trees, and Martens, following her eyes, considered the tower, its lime fire and massive lens, its beam that cut through the gloom of Danzig bay.

"No, not that," Martens said. His face was lost in the whipping about of his black hair. "Did you not see it? It was a light, sister, like a star brought low, as though the sky parted and let through a ray of heaven, and it fell," he said, raising and clasping his hands as though in prayer, "sister, it fell where you stand!"

The wind changed and revealed his face, a dark and drawn face with wide eyes, tears streaking from the corners.

"God reached for you, sister," said the lighthouse

keeper. "What did He say?"

God. In all of this, God had not occurred to Klara. She took a step back.

"It's difficult, I know," said the lighthouse keeper. "His way is obscure. I—I once heard him calling me! Can you believe it?" The lighthouse keeper smiled at Klara and came forward, plowing wet sand with his knees. "Do you want to know what he said?"

Klara backed further away.

The lighthouse keeper began to laugh. It was a panting laugh, revealing fear in his throat, a bit of a yelp.

He loosed his hands from their prayerful clasp and, laughing still, dug up wet, grey sand. It fell from his fingers. He looked across the bay. It was still dark, but only for a short while longer. A ship out there had already taken shape. Three bare masts.

"What is your name, sister?"

"Klara," she said, without meaning to.

Martens pushed back his hair, lacing it with the sand. He stood, stepping forward and brushing his knees, and said, "Klara. Sister Klara."

Klara had backed into the gunwale of a fishing boat. It was cold wood at the back of her legs. She reached back. Her fingers recognized the teeth of a clam rake's head, a heavy, slotted, iron mouth, and the moment her fingers closed on it, she swung it at the lighthouse keeper.

He fell, and she ran.

On the mornings that followed, Klara awoke in a variety of places: standing outside on the flagstone, then on the lane before the house, and again on the beach. Each time, she hurried back indoors, and her parents ushered her into bed, saying nothing. But then one morning, as Klara came back into the house after having awoken far out on the spit's single road, Klara's mother put her hand on the girl's shoulder.

The seam of Klara's nightdress was sticking up. It was on inside out and backwards.

Thereafter, her father bolted the doors. Klara again appeared on the beach. Her father nailed shut the windows. Once more, she awoke on the road, as if the stone and timber walls of her home were no more than curtains. Then, each night, Klara's mother tied herself to her daughter by strips of cloth at wrist and ankle. Yet Klara awoke alone in the woods. Her father organized a watch. Two men guarded the beach, two more stood by the road, and Klara's father and his brother watched the house.

After nights without incident, Klara appeared behind the men on the beach, causing one of them to shout in surprise. Neither had heard or seen her approach, nor had they dozed off. They had chewed horseradish roots to keep alert.

Klara's uncle had the notion to examine Klara's tracks. This was easily done, but in the end, six men wound up in the woods near the beach standing in a circle, bent at the waist, flummoxed. Klara's tracks began there. It was as if she had landed from the sky.

But then, tracks can be brushed away. They knew this because they had all been smugglers, a common job upon the spit.

Back at the house, Klara's grandmother, a small woman who had skin like a baby bird, declared an end to the talk. She led the girl to the bed, propped her up on the pillows, raised her knees, and parted her ankles. She stuck her thumb into Klara.

Grandmother pushed in all the way and arced her thumb from left to right. It was cold, and it hurt.

It didn't hurt enough, grandmother said. The girl did not bleed.

Some man, some demon, had robbed her of her virginity.

The man or demon had brushed away her memories of him, or rather snuffed her mind as one snuffs the flame of a candle. In her thoughts and dreams there was a void.

Once, when pressed by her parents, her grandmother and others, Klara recalled from the darkness of her thoughts and dreams the memory of a light. The light pulsed as though it were alive. It was the lamp of the demon that led her away from home. That's what the grown ups said.

The grown ups couldn't find a demon in Hel. They settled for Martens, the foreigner, the lighthouse keeper.

"I would not harm her!" Martens cried out as he ran from Hel.

Klara's father and uncles caught him on the road and beat him near to death. They broke his leg and cracked his head, I believe. Detectives arrived with Prussian writs of authority. Martens and the lighthouse belonged to a shipping company, a Dutch and Danish venture. Klara's parents sent the girl off of the spit to live a while on a farm belonging to an aunt named Hildegarda.

Two

Each morning Aunt Hildegarda took ink of blackberry and vinegar and painted crosses in the valleys between Klara's knuckles. She dried the ink with a whistling breath. Klara with her hands thusly blessed could help on the farm by pulling the last apples from the trees and the last turnips, carrots and potatoes from the dirt.

Aunt Hilde worked the field as if by rough gears wound up and set into motion. She was thin, almost disappearing against the white winter sky. Strands of her colorless, dark hair escaped from her headscarf and floated around her face.

One morning Klara awoke with Aunt Hilde screaming, "Back! Back into the forest, Satan!" It was now early spring and Klara was in the center of the field amid the black mud and strips of thin snow in the ruts. The hem of her nightdress was wet. Hilde was nearby, pointing to the treeline. "He flew," she cried. She seized Klara by the shoulder and said, "The Old One's found you."

Aunt Hilde took the girl back toward the house, and as Klara moved through the field, clods of dirt poked at the soles of her bare feet. The air was cold and fresh in her lungs, giving her a sting behind the eyes. Klara stammered, coming to, "You saw,

Aunt Hilde? You saw —"

"Don't speak his name, girl!" said Aunt Hilde. "We must get to safety."

There was no time to heat the water, so Aunt Hilde scrubbed the girl down with cold water just drawn from the well. Klara stood as her aunt worked her with a sharp scrub brush. She looked out the window and towards the trees beyond the fields. "He went yonder?" Klara asked, her chin juddering with the chill.

Aunt Hilde broke from her work for a moment. The trees were a low tangle against the pale sky.

"Yes," said Aunt Hilde.

"What did he look like?"

"He was no lighthouse keeper," said Aunt Hilde, resuming her scrub of the girl's legs. "I'll tell you only that."

Later, when Klara was dry and dressed, her aunt sat her at the table and laid the Bible between them. She cut blank pages from the end and wrote upon them.

"But if he comes again, shouldn't I know his likeness," Klara said, "so I can run from him?"

"He'll look any way he pleases," said Aunt Hilde.

Soon, Aunt Hilde had filled half a sheet of the Bible paper with a charm that read:

AbaxaCataBax

AbaxaCataBa

AbaxaCataB

AbaxaCata

AbaxaCat

AbaxaCa

Abaxa

Abax

Aba

Ab

A

She copied the charm many times over, each one to its own scrap of paper. She braided the charms into Klara's hair. She sewed them into Klara's clothes and into Klara's mattress. She buried them around the farmhouse and kicked the cold, wet earth back in place.

At noon, with this work done, Aunt Hilde and Klara stood in the field with their arms linked.

"The Old One was nearing you," said Aunt Hilde. "I came running," she said, "but he slowed me, he slowed everything, and he turned and flew."

Klara looked to her aunt. Her aunt had her jaw set and was squinting hard into the treeline.

"For a moment, he appeared as a deer," Aunt Hilde said, "as a stag, but then he was walking reared up like a man, and when he flew from you, he was bird, an owl perhaps, but he was so fast that he was more like a flame." There was admiration in Aunt Hilde's voice. "A white flame gone over the trees."

"Are you sure it was him," said Klara, "the Old One? And not something else?"

"I'm sure, my dear," said Aunt Hilde.

Klara followed her aunt's eyes. Over the trees, the Moon edged out from the pale blue, as though standing at a door half open.

On the farm, Klara missed the ocean but learned to sleep without its sound. She learned to enjoy the way the land absorbed the sky. She cared for the chickens, the pigs, the goats and the cow. In secret, she named and christened the animals with rapeseed oil, thumbing a crescent moon on their heads, even the cats in the barn, and even the seven dogs that followed her uncle, Hilde's husband, who was a mute named Piotr, around the farm.

One night, Klara awoke on her knees with her hair loose and the charms scattered on the floor in the moonlight. Smears of blood had dried down her thighs. Her skin and hair smelled of sulfur and iron. Aunt Hilde cleaned Klara and inspected her. "We know your tricks," Aunt Hilde said. She was speaking to Satan. "We know where you are hiding." Satan had hidden inside Klara, in her womb. "We will get you out."

On the following morning, Aunt Hilde captured a gray speckled dove, slit its throat and drained its blood into a cup. She bade Klara drink it down. The blood tasted of iron and dirt and was hot and smooth in her throat. Klara vomited the blood and everything else till from her lips drizzled a yellow foam that smelled of vinegar. Aunt Hilde stroked her back. Later, Klara could not stand. The ground kept tipping. Hilde wiped Klara's mouth and put Klara over her shoulder. She carried the big girl upstairs and flopped her onto her bed. Night and day went fast and slow as Klara suffered a fever and terrible stiffness. Aunt Hilde pried open Klara's mouth, pushed wadded bits of paper past her tongue, and sluiced them down with milk. Later, waking in the night, Klara found Bible pages on her chest. The pages were the latter half of *Revelation*. Her aunt had sliced the book out of the Bible and fed her the first eleven chapters.

By the moonlight, Klara read Chapter 12.

As best I can recall, the verses there say something to the following effect:

In the expanse of the sky, a woman appeared and was dressed in the light of the Sun. She stood upon the Moon and was crowned with stars. She was with child and cried out in pain. A red serpent came up from the Earth and threw a thousand stars down upon the mountains and plains. The serpent then opened its jaws to await the woman's child, but the holy infant spirited away to God, and the serpent turned on the woman. She sprouted wings and flew to a wilderness, a desert. The serpent, twice bested, vomited rivers to flood the world.

On a night soon after, Aunt Hildegarda knelt by Klara's bed and told the girl, "I have failed you." Aunt Hilde's eyes and cheeks were shining with tears. Moonlight was large in the room. Her hair was loose. White strands of it were illuminated. "But God has sent me word," she said. "He spoke to me through the cow."

"The cow?" said Klara. Ever since the fever, her own voice was low and loud in her skull. "The one in the barn?"

Aunt Hilde's voice sounded distant, as if she were a worried child calling from another room. "The Lord spoke in a voice without sound through the eyes of the cow," Hilde said.

"What did He say?"

"Only that it, the cow, could help, and that we should not be afraid."

The two of them put on their shoes. The Moon was full. The silver tops of the trees nodded and the entire field of potato blossoms, white and open in rows, shivered under a warm breeze. The barn as well was full of moonlight, and the cow—whom Klara had christened *Józefa*—was asleep on her side on her sandy bed. Her round flank rose and fell with breath. Her brown coat had a blue sheen. Hilde and Klara crouched to pray near the cow's head. The veins of its muzzle were moonlit.

What remained in the life of Józefa the cow was strange. It was summer. The cats erupted in hisses and baby moans in the night. Pigeons cooed in the barn's peak. Hilde and Klara slept above Józefa in a loft Piotr had framed. Each morning when Józefa got to her feet, Hilde and Klara climbed down and stripped before her. Józefa licked the salt from their bodies. The licking hurt. Her tongue was wide and strong and the women had to lean into it. Their ribs bowed under its muscle. When Józefa licked their throats, her tongue mashed all of those vital cords against each other. The texture was rough like a cat's tongue, and the saliva coated their skin as would egg white, and it gave off a boggy smell. Klara's body had a layer of fat for protection, whereas Hilde was all muscle, bone, vein and tendon under thin skin that, on each heavy stroke of the tongue, stretched. The skin went transparent over her ribs and the notches of her spine. Klara saw the blue roots of her aunt's blood.

After the licks, the women dressed. Hilde milked the cow and Klara dug a hole in a derelict field. Aunt Hilde would come into the hazy morning with a pail of Józefa's milk and pour it into the hole. The dark soil sucked the milk down, leaving just a tiny white puddle at the bottom. Klara filled the loosened dirt over it.

On the first morning of this ritual, Hilde entwined her fingers with Klara's and confessed that when she was a girl of thirteen, the Devil had visited her. He came as a tall man traveling out of the forest. His seed scalded out her womb, Hilde said. Klara had suspected as much. She loved her aunt and trusted that she meant no harm. Hilde kissed Klara's hand and said, "Whatever it takes, my dear, I will save you."

THREE

One night in August, the full Moon with its scars edged out from the trees and into the vibrant, darkening blue. Birds fled from one side of the field to the other. Fat ravens hopped along the potato rows and watched each other over the leaves. On the far side of the farm, in the wheat, a violet pool of fog gathered towards the woods.

Klara and her aunt were dressed in white. Józefa the cow was down and bound on a skid. Aunt Hilde stood over her with both hands on her muzzle. Uncle Piotr straddled Józefa's neck and sawed into her throat with a long knife. The cow screamed and thin streams of blood spurted. It took several more strokes before the knife silenced the cow, and yet more before it stilled the animal.

Attracted by the smell of blood, Piotr's dogs circled the cow. They swayed low on their paws and padded forward. Piotr bared his teeth, and the dogs slunk back with their tails between their legs, until once more the smell of blood brought them creeping forward.

Aunt Hilde's white dress, a rude covering that she had made that morning, was spattered with bright stripes of Józefa's blood. She was praying, asking God to pull the serpent from herself and

Klara, to bind it, crush it and cast it into the pit, to drive all leavings of Satan from them as wind would drive smoke. Blood spattered Klara as well. She stood beside her aunt and clutched a panel wood carving of St. Michael the Archangel. In the carving, St. Michael held a sword and shield. He was stepping on a man's neck.

Past the noise of her aunt's prayers and the cries of the animals, Klara heard a voice in the air. Likely it was only the caw of the ravens. They were flying from the field to the trees beneath the Moon.

Nearly two years had passed since Klara first went out in the night. Two years since she climbed the dunes near Hel and waited for who knows what. Klara had been a girl then, and now wondered whether she had imagined the spirits of that night, whether she had imagined the wolves and deer, the birds, the seals and the whales. The burning ship. Had she ever seen a light, pulsing as though alive?

"Klara, firewood," said her aunt.

Józefa was dead and they were going to burn her.

Klara followed her aunt around the barn to the wood pile. They took armloads.

All the strange nights since then, nights when she awoke out of doors, couldn't a natural phenomena lay at the heart of them? Klara used to read a primer on the physical sciences that her mother kept. It said that Odic forces, excesses of magnetism, roamed the world. At times this force moved people about like puppets.

Klara, Aunt Hilde and Uncle Piotr arranged firewood around and across the body of Józefa, and before long, a fire was lit, burning through the kindling with a funnel of grey smoke.

The Moon, by then, was a white eye with a shadow across it, and Uncle Piotr's dogs were whining, staring at the fire. The fire had the rich and acrid smell of Józefa's burning flesh.

"Take Saint Michael," Aunt Hilde said, putting the woodcut of the Archangel back into Klara's hands. "Pray with me."

Her aunt prayed. Her words were lost beneath the yelping of dogs and the crackling of the flames. Her aunt believed so much.

The breeze changed. Smoke from the pyre trampled over them, stinging their eyes and throats. The dogs were twitching, yelping and snarling. Their white teeth flashed in the smoke.

The heat of the pyre had Klara in a sweat.

"It's done now, dear," said Aunt Hilde

Uncle Piotr was swinging an axe handle, chasing his dogs.

Klara nodded, straightening up and wiping

tears from her eyes. Her aunt pulled her close.

"You'll be safe and sound," said her aunt.

"Oh!" said Klara, suddenly struck with an idea. "Aunt Hilde, perhaps I should see a doctor?"

Four

Klara asked the same of her parents one morning a few weeks later.

They had appeared outside the gate, standing in a borrowed cart, holding hands as Piotr's dogs whirled around them, barking. Klara kissed her aunt goodbye, walked through the dogs and boarded the cart. The dogs howled, Aunt Hilde cried praises—*You are my limb, Klara dear! My leg, my arm, God protect you!*—and Klara's father pointed the horse for Danzig, agreeing that a physician was in order.

They took a high road along a blonde valley of wheat. The mowers were out with their scythes, as were their wives, tying the bundles, disappearing beneath them and carrying them towards tall, dark shingled barns in the crib of the valley. The walls of towns, white as well, shone between the hills. The land flattened into an endless slope with stands of trees separated from each other by broad stripes of ashen ground. Beyond the trees, sunlight glinted off of long lines.

Train tracks, her mother explained.

As happens, the city closed around them, as though the towns had followed after them, creeping near and crowding out the distance of fields and forests, hills and all of the country. Gone were the long breezes that had traveled the world to greet them. In Danzig, Klara could only be where she was, on a bench beside her mother on a cart in a street between people and tall buildings with glazed windows. Then she was on a curb as her father haggled with a stable boy. Then she was crossing a square behind two women with blocks of ice on their backs, then stopping to let pass a team of black work horses pulling a cannon. Sparrows danced between the wheels. The frenzy and clamor, Klara found with surprise, was soothing.

All the noise and movement, it stood up between herself and her thoughts. Those spacious wonderings. Cut off now. Now out of reach. It was all Klara could do to walk. It was all she was called to do: to clutch her parents' arms as they went somewhere and waited, then follow them through a waiting room and into a doctor's quiet office, all glass, leather and polished wood.

The doctor was Kashubian like them. He was the first doctor Klara had ever seen. He wore a dark suit and stood with a bearing of calm. There were scales and glass beakers and shelves of books surely on bones and blood and what's beneath us all. He felt her wrists to read her pulse. He had large and warm hands. He settled in a chair and asked Klara to describe the *episodes*. He listened with a quality of attention that seemed to hear things that Klara could not. He then peered in her eyes and listened to her heart and lungs through a horn.

"No need to worry," the doctor said, having finished his inspection. "She's a sleepwalker."

"Sleepwalker," her father said to himself, and to his wife, "sleepwalker."

"Get her plenty of exercise, and avoid iron rich foods. Otherwise a normal life."

"That's all?" said her mother. Tears of relief hung in her eyes.

"Nothing more to it," the doctor said.

Her father jumped up and shook the man's hand.

"Wonderful!" her father said.

Klara stood from the examination table. At a loss, she curtsied to the doctor.

Her parents took her hands and they all passed back into the waiting room, which was full of patients. Her father paid the bill and got a receipt, muttering happily as he looked it over, "Wonderful, wonderful!" The doctor ushered them gently through the door and into the street.

A rogue storm had passed and left the city yet brighter.

From the rooftops, from pipes with dragon mouths, glittering chains of water fell. A knife vendor opened his coat, revealing the blades. Klara shielded her eyes from the shine. This was all a normal life.

"Klara," her father said, as though remembering a secret he had long wished to share, "I must show you something!"

Her parents took her into the stream of people, and brought her swiftly along the streets. Her parents, she saw, were neither rubes, nor backwards fisherfolk. Her mother was a city girl and her father a sailor who had seen Portugal. The two of them were glancing at each other with the proud and mischievous smile of Danzigers. They were lovely in their way. Her father was tall and dark and her mother was small and plump and fair, and Klara was both of them. The build of her mother and the height and color of her father. Klara was big, and she had always walked in apology of it, head bent and shoulders rounded, but not so today in Danzig. They entered a long, brick archway, and through it came the clean chill of the Baltic.

"You'll like this, Klara," her father said.

The sky opened and they came out to the quayside, the Motlawa, a broad river filled with ships.

The ships made another city, one of floating spires and heaving decks, a city lashed to itself and to cleats in the stone of the quay with ropes as thick as arms. People stood in the watery alleys between the hulls on log rafts with long poles. Gangways bounced with stevedores carrying sacks and crates. Sailors swung in the rigging. Passengers waved from the railings.

In Danzig, Klara would meet a young saloonkeeper named Louis Glockner. They would marry. He was bald and small and at their wedding he was twenty-eight. She was fifteen. Over the years her sisters came to stay. One married an Australian and sailed with him to the bottom of the world. Another married a man from Hel, but they migrated to Brazil. Klara and her husband Louis tried for years to have a child, but it came to nothing. One morning she confessed to him that when she was a girl, the lamp of the Devil brought her out in the night. The Devil knew her, everyone said. His seed had scalded out her womb. I cannot have a child, she said. Her voice shook. Her body shook. Louis, with his brow knitted and his mouth slack, stood from the bed and put a polite distance between them.

In the years that followed, the hope of having

a child faded in Klara as does a dream, one you can feel, but cannot remember. Klara would walk each morning along the quayside, that second city of ships that dispersed around the world and reformed, that city of bells, of seagulls. The cries of farewell, the blasts of horns and the smell of tar, iron, smoke and seawater, played within her that resonant strand, that mysterious and true feeling from her girlhood. Often as she walked the quay, she wondered about the consequence of her life, whether there was something she had forgotten.

Streams of men, perhaps myself among them, emerged from warehouse doors. We climbed the gangways onto ships and disappeared below. The Sun was between roofs, passing around the spars and masts on the water, and it lay its warmth on Klara.

FIVE

I was nineteen or twenty when I first saw Klara. Newly arrived in Danzig, I put my name down as an apprentice hand at the Seamen's Hall, calling myself Józef Nowak. I found work loading ships, instead. I drank through each mark I made. I took long rambles, used whores and slept in the leafy outskirts.

There was a beer hall attended by two pretty blondes. They darted back and forth with glass steins in hand. They flew through the stares of men, and as the night wore on, our adoration became dangerous. But step out of line and these sharp girls, with authority granted by the proprietor, would pitch a glass at your head. Then, in an instant, the doorman would appear with his fist wrapped in your shirt. Your stay was over. I never left in such a fashion, but I wouldn't stay long either. I liked the place, but it kindled in me a certain contempt.

There was also a small, near-empty dark cafe that had been a tailor's shop and still had the headless dummies lined against a wall. The barmaid had long, unpinned hair and a lisp that made her unintelligible. Service was slow. She never carried more than a drink at a time. She never met your eye. When she wanted you to leave, she'd lick her fingers and pinch out the flame of the candle at your table. On melancholy nights, after three or four drinks, her presence became beautiful and overwhelming. She moved as if walking underwater. I'd leave and wander the streets around Longmarket, trapped in the same ghostly pace.

One night when very drunk and full of shame, I went down some stairs to a basement tavern, a cave-like place. I got to a table and beheld Klara.

She seemed a fire, an unnatural stand of flames.

That impression is all that remains from that first night. I woke up beneath some bushes at dawn with that fire in my head as though I'd dreamt a scene from the wilder pages of the Old Testament. I went back a few weeks later.

Klara was lovely, strong and every inch herself. Her black hair was pulled back in braids. The gaze of her dark eyes cut level across the room. Her neck seemed to me majestic. She knew her trade. She strode the floor with six, eight or ten steins in hand. Just before the thought for another drink crossed your mind, the glass' bottom landed the very same ring of water your last glass had left. I remember the flush on her cheeks and throat and its reach into the neckline of her blouse. I remember the glance she'd give me as she wiped her hands on her apron, palms then knuckles. She was well into her thirties then, and she had seen thousands of me. I'd fall into my cups, discreetly glancing at her orbits. Lovely barmaids inspire cults, so I was not alone. But the cult of Klara was silent. To belong, one had to honor her indifference. Though, on occasion, less reverential drunks would fill a table. The lust and awe from these casual worshippers could turn to hate, as lust and awe often do, especially when the woman is the proud possessor of a body too large to manhandle. The hate was pathetic, like dead hatchlings on the ground. I would stay on guard and eyed these idiots with my fists clenched. Nothing ever happened. No lewd comments. None of them touched her. In the end, it was I that crossed the line.

My regard for Klara was beyond a drunkard's customary love of a barmaid, so it seemed to me at the time. In those days I worked hard and was belted with muscle. I cried at sunsets and wrote poems. Before her, I felt that I might bloom.

So, one night, when she was at the bar setting up glasses, I plucked up my nerve and approached her. I had decided to tell her my news, that I had finally gotten a job as an apprentice hand on a passenger line, a Dutch and Danish venture. I would soon ship out as a proper sailor.

As I neared the bar, she looked at me. I felt the thrill of magnitude one feels at the edge of a cliff.

"Miss Klara," I said, and before she could turn away in her duties, I declaimed a poem I had written her.

Here are the lines that matter:

I see a heart
It's dark like decay
Jewel-like with light
It's yours and mine
Over a wooded hill it waits
pulsing with far away lightning.

The poem came to me one morning as I woke up under a bush, and it played in my head all that day until I wrote it down on a packing slip.

I saw the heart in my mind's eye, as though it were a flame between us. I can see it now. It's bloody red, of course, but bright. It hovers within a diaphanous sack, a bit like a fist in a lace glove, and it beats, squeezing a trellis of veins that seize with light, but in a stutter, not a rhythm.

I also see the hill beneath it. Wooded in the rise, grassy at the foot, it's an oddly bell-shaped hill. A hill from Plato's mind. But this hill was a real and certain hill, a hill not far from where I was raised outside Bialystok, which leads me to believe that the vision of this poem comes from my childhood, from a day when I was perhaps dizzy from the summer heat and beheld the Sun low and angry behind a small, half-thick cloud, a sight my religious child mind took for a sacred heart.

This explanation satisfies me, but it fails to account for the shock the poem dealt to Klara that night in the tavern. Her eyes went wide, peering at me, and her face reddened.

I turned away.

One of my fellow worshippers, a respectful drunk, an old man who was a knot of muscle with a white beard and icy eyes, glared at me, outraged that I had broken our unspoken vow to never trouble her. Klara, our pagan queen.

I left the basement tavern and was soon crossing Longmarket, cursing myself. The tailor shop cafe was closed. I went to the beer hall, and it was a nightmare. The pretty blondes had multiplied and were flying around like finches. The sailors and stevedores and timbermen were bellowing, mustaches glistening. I drank fast in a corner alone. I raised my eyes, and one of the young barmaids was near, hiding from the crowded hall with her back to a pillar. She raised her finger to her lips. I nodded, and she smiled, then closed her eyes and tilted her head to rest against the pillar. I returned to my beer, my fourth, though it had no effect other than to fill me with bubbles. A while later, the feet of the stool beside mine squawked and the girl sat. She leaned against me and rested her head on my shoulder. She weighed nothing, a wraith of sweat. She laid a hand on my thigh and said, "Jus' lemme sleep a moment."

Of course, my body reacted, eagerly, though involuntarily, and my reaction stretched along my thigh. It pressed into her resting hand. She smiled, eyes closed.

"What's your name?" she said.

"Karl," I said.

Several men from the tables nearby were staring, but one with more rage than the others. He was round faced with sideburns and scarlet cheeks. His broad shoulders, tight against his red coat, were hunched up around his ears. His eyes hardened into pins. The scenario was clear: the sleepy, weightless barmaid was his girl, and she was using me to fire him up, or to keep him at bay, or both. If I sat there for too long, there'd be blood. Nevertheless, I sat a while, puzzling whether to sit for longer. The young lady squeezed me, as if to prime my strength.

I had a vision of the young man gutting me.

Just then another barmaid flew up to our table and started hissing at the one leaning against me, chiding her for drinking too much and for neglecting customers. They were nearly identical, certainly sisters, or at least cousins, and they began shouting at one another. I took the opportunity to walk out into the night.

There was a chill in the air. My skin tightened. Songs escaped from swinging doors. Other taverns were letting out with sailors, prostitutes and soldiers. Tramps proclaimed filthy jokes and reached out for alms. I came to the main quay, where ships jam the Motlawa. From the dark door of a waterside building, a girl with her long hair down stepped into the light of a streetlamp. She twirled an umbrella like a wheel upon the air. "You want some company?" she said.

My throat closed up with desire. I kept walking.

She fell in beside me. "Slow down," she said. "Look."

She unbuttoned the collar of her long coat.

I kept walking, crossing over the bridge. A wind blew down the Motlawa, through the chimneys, masts and spars. The ships moved. The thick ropes around the cleats squealed. The hulls rubbed on timber. A woman was close behind me. Perhaps the girl with the umbrella. She must be desperate, I thought. Available for cheap. I felt in my pockets for hidden coins and wadded notes. With relief, I found nothing. "I have nothing," I said. "I want nothing." I choked on the words.

In those nights, when I found myself in such a state of loneliness, of self-hate, want and lack, I'd walk out from the Eastern Gate of Danzig and go miles into the countryside until the city would huddle behind me in a mass of small darkness, and the meadows and the forest before me would open over silver, moonlit hills further south and east, nearer to where I was born. I'd stand on a rise hoping to hear the song of wolves in the forest. I made this walk often, but that night I didn't get far.

A woman called out to me, "Who told you to say that?"

It was Klara. She had followed me out of her tavern, into and out of the beer hall, and now raised white dust, walking toward me on a road beneath the Moon.

"My own heart told me!" I called, my voice in a yelp. I was shocked, of course, to see her, this tall woman, a figure coming closer, so shocked that I scarcely understood who either of us was. In my confusion, I heard myself shout, "I love you!"

The words halted her.

Oh, Klara by moonlight! Out of doors and in uncontained night, away from vaulted walls and the gold of lamplight and candles. So shattered my amber-tinted thoughts. Here she was. Here I was.

She said, "What do you know about me?"

"That you work in the tavern," I said.

"That's all?" she said.

"Yes," I said.

She stepped close. Her mouth was shut. Her nostrils flared. A blue sheen of perspiration silvered her throat. A loose shoot of her black hair was stuck in the sweat. She stared at me, staring as though reading for something written on the inside of my skull, and it didn't take long before Klara had looked into my eyes far longer than anyone ever had. It was terrifying. "When did you see the heart in the sky?" she asked.

"From a dream," I said.

Her eyes fell from me. She sighed—disappointment, or confusion, or both— and she turned and began walking back toward the city.

"May I escort you home?" I called. She gave no response, and I went after her, though I was careful to respect a distance in our steps.

After a while she said over her shoulder, "So, you're a drunk."

"Well, I'm a sailor, too, or will be," I said,

and thereafter I found it difficult to keep from jabbering further. "I'm shipping out on Saturday. My first time. To America. Philadelphia. Stopping in Copenhagen, Denmark, and Dublin, Ireland. Have you traveled, Miss Klara?"

"No," she said, and after a while she asked, "What's the ship called?"

"The Meteorite," I said.

"The Meteorite?" she asked.

"Yes," I said.

Further on still, yet before the city began again, she said, "Do you often wander out here at night?"

"What's that?" I said, hurrying to her side.

"I asked whether you often wander out here at night," she said.

"Yes," I said, "I do."

"Why?" she said.

"I like the forest."

She threw me a glance.

"I spent a lot of time in the forest where I'm from near Bialystok," I said. "I was in the Free Poland Militia," I said.

"Free Poland," she echoed. "You must be very brave. And very Polish."

"Oh, there was no real fighting. I joined too late for that. Mostly there was camping, some occasional fleeing. Most of it in the forest. I'm quite good at eating out of the forest. Mushrooms, birds. Trapping animals. Where are you from?"

"A fishing village," she said.

"What was it like?"

"Wet," she said. "Windy."

"Please, don't tell anyone that I was in the Free Poland Militia," I said.

"I won't tell," she said.

"I wonder whether I'm still so very Polish," I said, "in my heart."

Klara then slowed, letting me walk beside her, and an odd thing happened to the night. The hedgerows rippled. The smell of a cold stream came sharp through the trees. Even a horse pie on the road seemed to breathe. And I experienced these moments as if outside myself, as though my senses had become a ghost that ranged far from my body. "So," she said, "you're a poet."

"No," I said. "Just a drunk."

She smiled. Her cheeks still had the sheen of sweat. The strange sensation of the night ended. The stars and Moon laid light on our shoulders.

Before long, we came upon the city gate. The countryside was behind us, its meadows and forests forgotten, and our boots echoed as we walked beneath the old stone arch.

We came to the canals, which hold the best light

in the city, the reflection of streetlamps, a hundred rippling suns in the night. The merchant houses, tall and skinny affairs, had long since blackened their windows. We stepped upon the rise of a foot bridge. The canal gave off a smell of illness.

Klara stopped and sat on the low wall of the bridge. For a moment I was sure that she would fall back into the gliding black of the canal. It was a test, I thought, to see whether I would dive in after her. I braced myself to launch over the wall after her, ready to pierce the murk and current. Rats skittered below on the stone banks. Nothing happened.

"So you're leaving," she said.

"On Saturday," I said.

"On the Meteorite?"

"The Meteorite."

"Listen," she said. "I'm going to spend the rest of the night with you. But you must obey me."

"I'll do anything you ask," I said.

"You must never come back to the tavern," she said. "Do you understand?"

"Yes," I said.

Klara stood. She took my hand. Her fingers were cold. She held my hand tight for a moment, sealing a pocket of air the size of a robin's egg. Even thinking of it now, the sensation of it whispers in my palm.

We stole through the city. Its streets led us. The darkness was tall and clean. Moonlight flashed on the upper windows. Our footfalls raced over facades. We moved fast, as if falling. At a corner, Klara grabbed me by the face and kissed me. Our teeth, tongues and lips crushed together and opened a warm channel unlike anything I had ever experienced.

We arrived at a granary, a place where I had worked and kept the key, a place where I sometimes slept, a storehouse, flat-faced and hulking, six white-washed and black-timbered stories. I opened the door, we stole inside, and Klara let out a cry.

Watch-dogs stood taut in the moonlight and shadow. They licked my knuckles and Klara clutched my arm. We went up the stairs and the dogs squirmed around our legs. They waited for us with their heads cocked at the top of each flight. On the fourth flight, with the dogs observing a distance, Klara began to pull off her clothes.

A knife clattered to the floor, a kitchen blade that caught the moonlight. It had fallen from the folds of her skirts. For the second time that night, I imagined myself gutted, insides exposed. It would be worth it, I thought as I came towards her, tugging off my boots.

A pile of grain sacks made a massive, unforgiving bed. We fell into each other, tasting of salt, and the watch-dogs whined. Her body was curved, soft and strong. Her hands were hard and her sweat was cold. My heart was set to burst. That's how Klara and I began.

Six

In my drunken worship of Klara, I'd thought of her as a fire, a pagan goddess, unnatural and above me. But I was sober now, and we were both naked. She and I pressed against one another on the bed of grain sacks, both pretending to sleep. Our ribs rose and fell. My left arm went prickly then dead beneath her. We were joined in a way that was beyond my grasp, as though we shared a place of birth. This notion, a certainty, seeped through me. It was a painful seeping. Truly, it stung my psyche, my guts, for I so admired Klara that a certainty of our connection was a sort of self-regard, and self-regard is to my soul as salt is to a slug. Perhaps I squirmed. Klara pulled herself apart from me, rose and dressed in the purple darkness. The dogs and I watched. She said nothing. The dogs and I said nothing. Dawn was near and Danzig was waking. Klara, at the head of the stairs, said, "Stay."

We obeyed, and she disappeared into the floor, her heels clicking on the stair treads. The dogs whined, then scrambled to peer down after her, jostling each other and scraping their nails on the wooden floor. The door closed, four flights down, with a faint thud.

That granary was Kotlowitz & Sons, and like all Danzig granaries it existed on an island within the city where no one, for fear of fire, was permitted in the dark hours. A few years later, a spark rose in the heat trapped in the upper stories of that granary, or a granary nearby, and much of the island caught fire. The canals around the island, I'm told, filled with swimming dogs.

Once, after my adventure with Klara had ended, I was alone in Texas and walking through a day that got darker and darker in a brown haze. At night, blind, I crested a ridge. The wind changed and revealed a valley consumed by fire. The low mountain nearby had burned and the remaining flames made a field of red stars. The smoke came running over me, and I crawled back down the ridge in the blackness. I believed I was dead.

I don't know where, when, or to whom I was born. My first memory is of walking in a hallway and breaking my pinky toe on a flagstone that had come up. Monks raised me, and the abbot of the monastery once told me that my father died before I was born, and that our home was seized to settle debts, leaving my mother to give birth in a stable and abandon me at the monastery. So you see, the abbot said, your mother was a bit like Mary, but without Józef. That's why I named you Józef, he said. Every orphaned boy in the abbey was named Józef. Respectfully, I raised this issue to the abbot. Yes, well, all foundlings have a similar story, he said, but then a shadow of confusion crossed his face, as if he realized that he had mistaken me for another boy Józef, and that the story he told me was not my story at all. Aside from orphans, monasteries are dumping grounds for the imbecilic sons of the rich. These degenerates go on to become abbots and teachers and otherways masters to us orphans, who are slaves of the order. I was such a slave, one that learned several languages and exquisite penmanship, but a slave nonetheless, and because I was strong and had a talent for suffering, I farmed the grounds.

One morning, I escaped the monastery and joined the Free Poland Militia in a field outside of Bialystok. They were a dozen men with sabres and rifles, feathers, pins and tassels, muddy tents, red scarves, black boots, billowing trousers and great mustaches. They were old. The January Uprising was an age ago. But I didn't see the rust on their weapons or the dye in their beards. To me they were heroes, though I had never before considered Poland. I did all that they asked and never grew tired of their tales of women, gunsmoke, blades and nooses. They enjoyed having me around.

As befits the bearers of a lost cause, they had a religious zeal that would put the monks to shame. Our captain, for example, refused a map and compass, and instead reckoned his way through the forest with prayers to the Virgin. They made me a scout. We harassed the little Russian garrisons along the Neman and Bug Rivers. One afternoon, after a summer of stealing their goats and chickens, blocking their roads and setting fire to their walls, the Russians got annoyed and came out to kill us. At the time, I was on lookout, and I spotted a Russian squad on the east side of a wooded valley. Just as soon, another squad of Russians came into the valley from the west. I ran down to our campsite to warn my aging comrades that we'd been trapped, but they had already scattered. I reached their fire and stood alone by its banner of smoke. A hole opened in the dirt before my feet. The Russians had proper rifles that could brain a man at three hundred paces. I ran, and bits of bark and dirt exploded around me. A day later in the town of Zabrow, a priest hid me in the church beneath the stand of votive candles. He ordered me to pray. I obliged him, or attempted to, but could think only of my forehead and knees on the cold, hard stone, the hiss and crackle of the candle wicks above me, and the echoes in the altitude of the church's apse. I wept with lonesomeness. I wept for myself, my comrades, the Józefs back in the abbey, and for my mother and father, dead or alive, gone at any rate. Later, I walked east and north and got work on a timber barge drifting up the Vistula. The barge belonged to an Austrian widower who named it The Mother Mary. He'd stuck a shrine to Our Lady on top of the pilot house. Her cloak once had jewels of colored glass, but thieves had chipped them out. As a child, I would talk to a Black Madonna in the monastery. I would weep and weep. That Madonna was as close as I had to a mother. Years later in Danzig, when such lonesomeoness struck again and drink and whores could not blunt it, I would climb to the top of a granary and sway at the edge over the black cobblestone below. Fear of becoming a ghost kept me from killing myself, fear that I'd go on as a being of pure want.

On the dawn after my night with Klara, I had to abandon my boots at Kotlowitz & Sons. They were lost somewhere in the sacks and daylight was fast approaching. I stole out, careful of the watchmen in their rounds. With my bare feet on the stones of Danzig, I felt myself a different creature, an animal set loose.

That morning I went to see the captain of the Meteorite, the ship to which I was bound.

"Mister Nowak," he said, "good to meet you."

His office was disorienting. The light fell in extremes, blaring from a skylight while darkness stood undisturbed in the corners. The captain was standing in the light and arranging papers on his desk. He leaned forward and back, and again, and as he did, his stiff coat gave him the look of a tolling bell. At length he took off his coat and cap. The cap he set on his desk, and for his coat, Mister Reich, the boatswain, a small man with a trim beard, appeared with a hanger.

"Sit, won't you, Nowak?" the captain said.

I sat, and with that the captain took his seat behind the desk. He squinted at me and said, "Very well." His name was Langobard. He was English, or French, or Swiss. He struck a clean picture. A white-haired man in his realm. The cabin walls were polished wood panels, and each panel had a framed picture at its center. Two lamps were nailed to the corners of the desk, and their glass chimneys, though unlit, shone livid white with daylight. The captain nudged his cap, moving it an inch over on his desk.

"First time as a sailor, Nowak?"

"Yes, sir."

"These days, on a commercial ship at least, a sailor is shod as he moves about."

"Sorry, sir. I've lost my boots."

Captain Langobard frowned and tapped his thumbs together. "Reich, did you hear? Nowak needs boots."

"I did, sir. Indeed he does, sir."

"See that he gets a pair, would you, Reich?"

"Aye-aye, sir."

"Reich here tells me of your reputation in labor, that you toil like a ... what was it, Reich?"

"Like a slave to Pharaoh, captain," said Reich.

"That's good," the captain said. "A slave to Pharaoh. Fitting, as you're a Semite."

"No, sir," I said.

"No?" he said.

"Yes, sir."

"Yes, you're a Semite?"

"No. Yes, I'm not a Semite, captain."

"Yes, well, you're rather too tall for that. Either way you'll need boots."

"Yes, sir."

"Reich will locate a pair," he said. "Reich's a Semite. A Jew."

I nodded.

The captain leaned back in his chair and nodded at me. "Well then. You wanted to see me?"

"Yes, sir. I'm resigning my post." I had decided in my transit across the city that morning. I would stay in Danzig and win Klara's heart. The whole of me felt weightless. I had to fight a smile from breaking out across my face. Within moments, I'd be free. Gulls would soar and scream over me. I'd have an apple for breakfast.

Captain Langobard narrowed his eyes. "Is it a woman?" he asked.

I answered without shame, "Yes, sir."

"She knows that you're a sailor and that you're set to depart?"

"Yes, sir," I began, "she —"

Langobard raised a hand and continued: "Nowak, you've only just met this woman, correct?"

"Well, yes, sir," I said. "I've only just gotten to know her."

"And what do you know about her, Nowak?" he asked.

I muttered something about a fishing village, and Langobard nodded. He gestured to nudge his cap, but didn't actually touch it. He then leaned forward into the light. His face was thin. Its lines were numerous and fine. In a low tone, he spoke:

"I am not a priest, Nowak. Nor a rabbi. I've no

parochial qualms. I've sailed to all far reaches of this world and witnessed how living is done. What's more, for decades I've observed a revolving set of men, the crew, close at hand. It's been an education in mankind, Nowak. An education. Mister Reich has had the same privilege. Correct, Mister Reich?"

"Aye, sir," said Reich from the darkness.

"One develops a realist's view of this animal called man," Langobard said. "And, the animal that man calls woman. Now, you and this woman—" He tapped the desk. "—You've consummated this new love, correct?"

I could only nod.

"In fact," he said, "she treated the consummation as a matter of some urgency?"

"Yes, sir," I said, realizing with a sickening drop that Langobard had gone through this scenario with many a fool sailor. The melody of my heart was an old tune lifted from a worn out songbook.

The captain snapped his fingers.

"Stay with us, Nowak. I'm afraid we're getting to the heart of the matter."

The Sun lit up his white eyebrows. In the shade beneath them, his eyes floated. "Now, Nowak," he said, "she did not ask you to come here and surrender your post, did she?"

"No, sir."

"Well, I can tell you she won't like it, Nowak. She wants you on this ship. She wants you earning a wage. You see, my boy, it's a swindle."

Langobard leaned back. He tugged at his cuffs and held up a hand. "You're skeptical," he said. "Allow me to offer a few predictions for you to test as time goes on."

I nodded, at what I wasn't sure.

Langobard cleared his throat and proceeded: "You'll find that on Friday next, the day before launch, she'll come to you bearing some rather important news. You follow, Nowak?"

"Aye, sir." I did not follow.

"There'll be a tearful goodbye, promises of fidelity. You'll sail and eight weeks later return to find that she has grown in a very localized manner. Understand?"

"Yes, sir." Again, I did not.

"You'll sail once more, this time leaving your advance wages with her. That's key, Nowak. A few more trips to America and back, and sure enough, there she is at the foot of the gangway with an ankle biter, all swaddled up for you to hold."

"Ankle-biter, sir?"

"Yes, Nowak. A gift from God. An infant," Langobard said. "On that day, you're a man, a father, and a proper sailor to boot. Congratulations." He nodded to Reich somewhere behind me.

"Happened to me, sir," said Reich.

Langobard nodded, now with solemnity, and leaned forward once more. "You see, Nowak, thus is made a family man."

"I see, sir."

"It happens to the best of us. The very best."

"Yes, sir."

"And why not? Have you something better to do? For Christ's sake, it happened to Reich!" the captain said, raising a fist into the light.

"Yes, sir."

"And no shame in it. No looks askance to this woman. She has her future and the future of her infant to think of. We're not innocents, priests or rabbis. We're not parochialites! This is how living is done, Nowak." He thrust a finger at me. "Though you're in your rights, my boy, to deny her," he said. "It is a swindle after all. A sham. The infant is not yours. Not if we're speaking technically, physiologically. It won't have your curly hair, nor your …" he gestured up and down "… your height."

"My firstborn looks like the baker down the lane, sir," said Reich.

Langobard erupted in laughter and banged the desk with his fist. "A sailor's lot," he said. "Eh, Reich?"

"Indeed, sir," said Reich.

Langobard knuckled away a tear and sighed. "Then it's settled. New boots and a baby for Nowak. He honors his contract, remains in the employ of this vaunted shipping venture —" He clapped his hands, remembering something. "— But in a new station, upon the boatswain's recommendation. That's correct, Mister Reich?"

"That's right, sir."

"Now, I understand that you wanted to be up in the rigging, Nowak. Like a true sailor of yore. But it's no good. You're too tall, and there's no future in it. The dawn of the machine and all that. One day, and soon, no ship in the company fleet—nay, upon the sea itself—shall hang a sail. The engines will do all the work, and that's where we'll put a strong young lad like you," said Langobard. "The engine."

"Yes, sir, Captain Langobard," I said. "The engine."

"The furnace to start," said Captain Langobard. "You're a fireman now, a stoker."

Reich sent me to the coal hold, a metal room deep in the ship. At the far end, a chute was open and daylight came in as a square beam. Three men huddled by this light. I made my way over, bent from the low ceiling, and one of them handed me a shovel.

At once, the light ceased and in came the coal.

It roared, cascading upon the metal floor. Dust flew up and I reeled back. Over the din, someone shouted words I couldn't understand. A hard hand grabbed my collar and shook me. Another man came to my aid, shouting in my ear. "Each man has a corner!" he said, pointing to mine.

The work was hellish. The four us threw all we could manage to our respective corner, thusly spreading the fuel. A floor of coal rose up. The ceiling pushed down on our shoulders, then spines. Soon we had to crawl on the blockish, sharp field. Sparks fluttered around my air-starved mind. For long stretches, I entered an automatic, insensible state. Moving, struggling for breath, moving until the fuel slowed, then stopped.

We were on our knees, backs to the ceiling. We did not delay, but scrambled out of the hatch to the furnace room, one after another, dragging our shovels, coal tumbling after. We crouched and coughed, hocking out a black slurry. Dry pellets of coal came from my nose. The last fireman emerged from the hold. He was the chief, the one who had grabbed me. His name was Marcel Dudko. He was two white eyes in the black plane of a head.

SEVEN

In the days that remained, I honored my orders from Klara and stayed away from her tavern. Instead, I was a slave to the Meteorite and prayed that Klara would find me and deliver me, swindle or no.

Saturday morning arrived, passengers came aboard, and the ship's whistle blasted. We the crew undid the ropes from the cleats of Danzig's quay and wound them up into the capstans. We pulled the anchors from the Motlawa's silty bed. The whistle blasted several times again and steam wreathed the sidewheels. Pistons took up their rhythm in the belly of the ship. The sidewheels cut the black water into froth.

The Meteorite was six decks from the hold to the pilothouse and seventy long strides from bow to stern. The ship trembled from its iron hull and through the four timber masts. It rattled the rings on the flagpoles and the wine glasses hanging in its sunlit restaurant. We moved from the stone and wood of the city's watery edge. On the main deck, the first class passengers waved goodbye. From the stern, steerage passengers did the same. In degrees, most all wore a look of shock.

After a while, less than an hour, the roofs

of Danzig disappeared around a bend, and the passengers turned to each other and the ship, this bit of the land escaping the land. Life is odd.

The Meteorite took the easternmost tine of the delta into the bay. The winds favored us. Each sail opened with a snap, and before evening we were on the Baltic proper.

I worked at night in the fireroom, shoveling fuel from the coal hold and into the four doors of the furnace. One could watch the gauges, or wait for the engineer's shout through the speaking tube, a metal cone that hung by your head. The engineer wanted either more, or less. Your job was secure, so long as the fire stayed in the furnace and you didn't pass out from the heat, dust and strain.

Stoking suited me. I lost my lovelorn self in the swing and bite of the shovel, the sweat and erasure of the heat. I'd rake the coal embers even, watch them flare as they tumbled. Oh, the flames. Weightless and hungry. How right a bed of them!

But one couldn't stoke for long. In those days a fireman would shovel for three quarters an hour and take rest in the fourth. A hand from somewhere in the ship would relieve you, and they were none too eager for the job. The toil of the fireroom had a peculiar strain. You left it unsure of your steps, as though the furnace had singed back the nerves that held the world straight.

You were all sweat and ache.

I found cure in the open air. At each rest, I'd make my way up to the foredeck, and Lord, the shock! The wind would buffet me up onto the balls of my feet so that I could lean against its power, and it would grip me back together by driving its icy blades to my core. Through wind-spurred tears, I'd look at the sea and sky.

Intimations of eternity are awful.

One night, ten days into the voyage and several hours after pushing off from Dublin, Ireland, an apparition passed over the ship.

I did not behold it, not precisely, and so can only relate the great confusion caused by the apparition, or whatever it was.

Shortly before it appeared, I was taking in the night air on the foredeck as was my habit, and I recall storm clouds of thick and dirty silver attending the horizon.

The sight of clouds at sea, I couldn't master it. They were as lost and strange as we, I thought; such was my condition—a heartsick but hopeful boy, battered by the wind and in a trance of clouds— when suddenly the Moon appeared before the ship.

I mean to say that at one moment, there was nothing.

No Moon. Just the ocean. Dark beyond itself. An inverse of illumination.

And in the next moment, there was the Moon. Large and laying down a path of light. Thrown just off of the bow. It wore a single star as a pendant.

Stunned, perhaps frightened, I made my way back, passing beneath the pilot house, a high glass cabin aglow with lamps, when a door slammed. From the top of the ladder a man shouted to me, "Sailor, did you see that?"

It was Adem Martens, the lighthouse keeper from Hel, a man mistaken for the Devil. I knew him then as the ship's carpenter. He was gripping the railings, feet set apart.

"You mean the Moon sir?" I cried back.

He lowered himself a few steps, regarding me. The Moon was at his back. The center of his face was dark. "What's your name?" he asked.

"Józef Nowak," I told him, adding, "I'm in the furnace," as an explanation as to why I'd never traded a word with him. The Meteorite was a steam and sail ship. Martens, as the ship's carpenter, was an attendant to the masts and spars and sails, whereas I toiled for the engine. I had, however, seen Martens before. He worked alone and at all hours, rattling around with a long, black box of tools, moving with a hop in his step. His spine curled him over, as though bowing for the lash. Later, I'd hear the scuttlebutt that he was Boer from southernmost Africa, and that on his first voyage he dove into the South China Sea to save a child gone overboard. The child belonged to a principal stockholder, it was said, and Martens had since labored thirty years in the shipping venture. Company regs didn't apply to Martens, they said. To wit: he made his bunk beneath the bench of his shop, and he wore no cap and never cut his hair.

That hair, whipping in the moonlight and wind, gave him the look of a madman.

"I have to get back to the furnace, sir," I said.

He remained at the top of the ladder, gripping the railing. I went on toward the stern, unnerved, yet the strangeness would deepen, for upon the steerage deck a group of Irishers stopped me.

We had rounded "Malin's Head" that evening, and all night the Irish passengers had huddled in a range of dark coats, caps and shawls against the stern railing, giving off waves of feeling while they watched their land vanish. But now they were shouting and wailing.

They had seen something.

An Irishman clapped me on the chest. He had

large teeth and rheumy eyes. He was jabbering, terrified, but I had not a word of either English or Irish. Another man, this one in a bob hat and spectacles, pulled him back, and to my surprise I understood that this bespectacled Irishman was insisting one word to me and to his countryman: "Albatross!" he said. "Albatross!"

"Albatross?" I said, making a bird with my hands.

The bespectacled Irishman nodded, making his own bird of hands.

Albatross. The great gull's name flies unchanged across several languages.

Then, a steward called Tommy Fay, an Irisher himself, came onto deck to calm the crowd, and in a moment he turned, his eyes now wild as well, to ask me in German, "Did you see it? Did you hear it?"

"See what?" I asked.

Fay then explained to me the spirit the Irish call "Banshee."

"She's a fairy woman that flies about screaming when there's a death," he said.

I understood immediately, for as a child I was terrified of the "Strzyga," an owlish demon that did the same in Polish forests.

"Bosh!" cried the spectacled Irishman, repeating again, "Albatross!"

The reader may know that the albatross is a stranger to the North Atlantic. I was ignorant of that fact, and instead imagined that the bespectacled man was correct. The Irish, I imagined, had been at the railing in a shared trance of melancholy when a terrifyingly large and white seabird rose up in the draft of the Meteorite's stern.

Seabirds as they climb on the air have always reminded me of Christ crucified.

One woman, a stricken thing with clear eyes and an infant in her shawl, was shouting at the bespectacled man and Fay and then me.

"Is she saying *angel*?" I asked Fay.

He nodded.

Enough, I thought. Moon, albatross, banshee, angel! I hurried below deck for the furnace, and there the strangeness took one last step.

"Where in blazes have you been?" cried the engineer that had relieved me. "You've been gone for hours!"

He dropped the shovel to the ground and staggered by me. The smell of sick was thick in the heat. The engineer, I realized, had puked his supper across the floor. I must have, I reasoned, dozed on my feet while on my break at the foredeck. That would explain the jump of the Moon. But such a thing seemed impossible. Could I have made my repose on a mattress of wind?

As punishment for my dereliction, no one relieved me for the remainder of my shift and I shoveled myself into delirium. Dudko, the chief stoker, came to me in the morning. He slapped me on the head.

In my dizzied state, I hadn't seen him enter.

"Nowak!" he said, thrusting forward a rectangular object. "You've neglected the ash boxes!"

He dropped the ash box on my feet and a cloud of its grey powder raced up the length of me and into my mouth, nose and eyes. The head stoker then went about swearing oaths and throwing ash boxes. There were eight all together. "Don't neglect the ash, Nowak!"

Under Dudko's glare, I was another hour tidying the fireroom. He bid me out with a kick, and I crawled up the ladders and through the passages to the crew's cabin. I washed up and tried to sleep.

Ship berths were never intended for men of my dimension. The crown of my head pressed hard to the corner whilst my toes and knees were crammed against the wall. The seaman that occupied the berth at night, Oppel was his name, gave off a musk of leather and tobacco. Pleasant enough in person. However, this musk of his had become concentrated in the pillow and sheets, as did the tang of his sweat and the baywater stench of his breath and farts. As my body was already sickened by the heat of the furnace, Oppel's miasma became unbearable. It weighed on my face and throat. Worse, most all the other sailors were just starting their day. They rustled through the bunks and pounded up and down the ladder. They pissed their morning stream into the head. Add to this the flow of voices, the passengers on the main deck above me, their words on the wind. I was victim to dreadful hallucinations:

I saw the black and steady eyes of an albatross, which was also the Strzyga and an owlish Christ. At one point, the curtain of my berth parted, and there stood a man. His head blocked the light and I took him for a dream. I believe it was Martens.

Eight

I believe it was Martens because he thereafter took an interest in me. One morning he stopped me in a passageway, holding up his black box of tools, and asked whether I'd like to apprentice to him as ship's carpenter. "Honor your namesake, boy," he said, "Christ's earthly father." He rattled the tools. "It's your calling."

"Thank you, sir," I said, "but I cannot. The captain has obliged me to the furnace."

True, I had hoped to learn of sailing and ships, and in the fireroom I would learn nothing. I had, however, already grown fond of my job; I enjoyed the solitude and the annihilations, both at the furnace and in my breaks on deck against the wind.

But it wasn't my aptness for my lot that bade me turn down Martens' offer, for I am accommodating to a fault and will swallow whatever disgusting gruel is offered. I turned Martens down because I feared him.

I feared him in an animal way, as one fears heights and spiders.

He was looking up at me. A dull shine showed a ridge in his crown, as though it had once been cracked open. He had, I imagined, witnessed the stuff of his own mind. His eyes, glimmering from within scaly folds, testified to it. They were eyes borrowed from a face both older and younger. Looking into them, I withered.

"Very well, Nowak," he said. "Back to your station then."

Martens wasn't done with me. When we docked in Philadelphia, he asked Reich to assign me as his helper with repairs. I had hoped to explore the American city, but found myself on the dock beside the strange carpenter, the two of us painting the portside hull with brushes on long poles. Fortunately, as one would not paint over the other's work, the chore moved us in opposite directions along the iron skin of the ship. Often throughout the day, however, he'd close the distance between us on the dock and observe my work, standing at my elbow, until at last he'd back away and return to his own brush and pail of green paint. By dusk, a long portion of the hull was refreshed, and Martens and I stood beside each other, cleaning our brushes with turpentine.

To our backs, the falling Sun blotted out Philadelphia. Across the plain of the Delaware River, the warehouses of Camden darkened. Our day of silent and symmetrical work had given Martens a channel into my psyche. Or perhaps it was the atmosphere of the moment, charged as it was with the clean fume of turpentine, purpling light and a river's breeze. Either way, he related to me a scene that occurred at once in my mind's eye:

"When I was a lad and sailing on the Arabian Sea," he said, "our pilot took us through a rainbow."

"Through?" I asked.

"Yes," he said. "Its colored beam traveled the deck, right over where I was standing."

"The beam fell upon you?" I said.

"More than *fell upon* me, I'd say. It electrified me, Nowak."

"How do you mean, sir?"

"I mean I was both chilled and burned at once, and by some miracle the rainbow lifted me by half a foot from the surface of the foredeck."

Upon my face, I suppose, was a look of dueling credulity and skepticism. While I knew, as Aristotle and Descartes had shown, that rainbows stay forever on the horizon as plays of light and water, I believed Marten's tale, as well. He was telling the truth.

The man was nothing but truth. He had been ground by the millstones of the sea and sky and had lost all his chaff. He was at the germ of the human grain. So it seemed to me.

He took my brush and said, "It's clean. Off you go, Nowak."

I left the dock, but the puzzlement he inspired in me survived several drinks in a saloon. On the next morning, when I, suffering from a terrible bottleache, reported to him on the dock to continue our job of painting the hull, he had gained the look of a prophet.

A prophet of a faith that was not mine, but a prophet nonetheless.

We set to our task with our brushes on poles and pails of green paint. By the nature of the work, we were yet farther apart than the day before, and so when he'd close the distance of the dock to stand at my elbow and observe my work, he was a full minute or two in his silent approach, the river blazing behind him.

On one of these visits, I asked him:

"What did you make, sir, of the incident of the rainbow?"

"What?" he said.

"When the rainbow traveled upon the deck and electrified you, sir."

"Oh," he said, "the rainbow was the Holy Ghost."

The answer embarrassed me, and I directed my gaze to the hull, to the fresh stripes I had laid upon the faded green.

"Has the Holy Ghost ever made itself plain to you, Nowak?" he asked.

"No, sir."

"Well, you're in luck," Martens said, "for here in America, the Holy Ghost often makes itself plain."

Martens had been gazing upon the hull, as well, but I felt my skin tighten. I knew that he had turned his glimmering eyes to me. "Shall I take you to meet the Holy Ghost?" he said.

I lowered my paintbrush and braved a look at the man. The sunlight was bouncing against the water and coming up through the slats of the dock to gild him from below.

"The Holy Ghost appears nightly in Philadelphia. I'll show you."

"Sounds perilous, sir," I said, attempting a joke.

Martens shook his head.

"There's but one trick to it," he said. "To meet the Holy Ghost, one need only to know one's own soul."

For a moment as this odd, golden man stared at me, my bottleache redoubled. A sweat broke out across my body, the sort that precedes vomiting.

"So, Nowak," he said, "shall we meet the Holy Ghost this evening?"

I said, "Aye, sir."

Thus I wound up in a makeshift church that night, or rather in a stream of a few hundred Philadelphians with Martens as my guide, making our way to a grand tent on a lot at the scattered northern edge of the city. The atmosphere was rather more carnival-like than churchly. A catherine wheel spun on a high pole by the entrance, raining red, white and blue sparks on our heads. A vendor hawked oysters and eel. On a corner by the lot was a saloon, and its keeper beckoned to the crowd from his stoop, pointing to a table set upon on the curb. It was resplendent with full glasses of whiskey and beer. Indeed, the Philadelphians paid the keeper two bits a glass—an outrageous price!—and guzzled down the drinks. A one-man band stomped around on the grassy edge of the lot. A dancing bear would not have been out of place. Lamps blazed within the tent. The congregation, such as it was, elbowed in and pushed towards a stage at the far end. I tried to stay towards the back—a tall man is despised in an audience—but Martens pulled me forward. The show began when a wild-looking man climbed the stage.

He was the first of three preachers for the night, and seemed as though he had arrived from the wastes of the Holy Bible. His eyeballs were silver, consumed by the mercury of cataracts. He was dressed in an oversized brown coat, ragged at the seams. He held both hands up to the crowd and began his preachment. I, of course, understood very little, but I admired the commitment of his speech; for half an hour he shouted without cease. His hands did not waver.

The crowd, however, became restless. People through the audience grumbled and soon turned to each other to complain. The man went on shouting, holding his hands in the air as though pressing a barrier. He was alone, trapped in his mercury. The crowd's complaints grew to jeers, drowning out the poor fellow until at last someone escorted him off of the stage and to the far corner of the tent, where he sat alone, appearing all the wilder for the wide berth the crowd gave him. There were some announcements, during which men came through with collection baskets. The Philadelphians emptied their pockets. And then the second preacher ran upon the stage.

The congregation cried out, and at first, I took it as a cry of derision.

This preacher was ridiculous. A young man in shirt sleeves and a vest, he was soon red in the face and slick with sweat. He paraded the stage, singing and shouting out his preachment, until, in a moment of great applause, he beat his chest like a bass drum and wailed, "Jesus! Jesus!" spurring the crowd to take up the chant, whereupon he rolled his head about his shoulders. The bizarre gesture provoked the crowd, for it portended something, and as he rolled his head ever faster, the chant of "Jesus! Jesus!" broke into wild cries that carried, I'm sure, far past the canvas of the illuminated tent and into the night of Philadelphia's trashy edge.

This couldn't last, I thought. Surely the crowd, which had shown itself hard to please, would harass this bunko man from the stage. But then the preacher, this hysteric, stopped in his tracks. The crowd went silent. With the sudden quiet, a shiver spread among the audience, like a forest before a storm. All at once, the preacher cried out, and the shivers became spasms. Ladies lost their bonnets. Men lost their hats. Combs and eyepieces flew and were soon underfoot. The crowd flailed. A woman's knuckles struck me in the face. To escape, I swept aside one shuddering man and another and another. At the exit of the tent, I stopped and watched a few hundred people convulse. A man near me, jerking and twitching on his feet, tried to leave it, but fell back into the froth of limbs and faces as though lassoed.

Throughout my life—in the monastery, in the woods with the patriots, at Easter parades and elsewhere—I've often witnessed scenes of religious transport. Each time, I've found myself marooned. I sit alone with an indifferent God while others traffic to a realm to which I have no entry. There are fakers and frauds, but how can I know what's true?

The preacher was holding up a Bible, pantomiming a tug-of-war with the sky. The sight of him, his absurdity, allowed me to turn away.

I left the tent and stood on the curb by the saloon. A number of its patrons were on the stoop. They were listening to the madness and watching the tent. A mass of shadows washed around its canvas walls. The saloon patrons shook their heads, in amazement or disdain. I handed over some coin and drank from the whiskey on the curbside table. It was awful stuff. Two fellows, Irishers or Scots, both with great mustaches and sidewhiskers, questioned me about the goings-on in the tent. I explained that I spoke little English, and they nodded, but then shrugged and talked at me nonetheless. They were friendly and put across that they worked in a hat factory. I mimed that I was a sailor, an engine stoker. "Look," one said to the other, pointing. A man stood by the entrance of the tent. He was stripped to the waist and wearing a black hood over his head. "That's Jim," one of the

Irishers or Scots said to me. He added—I believe—
"He's me wife's brudder."

Jim was a penitent of some sort. He began to
whip his bare back with a scourge of knotted rope.

The Irishers or Scots passed me another whiskey.
The keeper, who was on the stoop as well, waved off
the payment. Under the stars and clouds, breathing
in the stink from a nearby trash pile where a pig
was rooting, I stood with these makeshift friends,
watching a brother-in-law mortify his flesh while
the Holy Ghost raged through hundreds of bodies
in a brightened tent.

Philadelphia. It has a certain charisma.

"You," one of the fellows said to me, "you have
a wife?"

Here was my first full sentence in the English
language, and it was a lie to boot: "Yes, I have a
wife."

A little man in a beret and long coat rounded
the corner, and the keeper grabbed glasses from
the curbside table, muttering oaths. The little man
neared, his face twisting in a goblin's smile. The
fellows made me to understand that we had to get
the glasses inside, lest this little man reach them,
and so I was soon through the doors of the saloon,
arms laden with glasses sloshing beer and whisky
down my shirt. The little man peered in from the

door, but stayed there, as though the threshold were enchanted against his entrance. The keeper treated me another drink for my troubles. I lost the two friendly fellows in the dark line of men at the bar, and then I remembered Martens, and so after a few more drinks I left the saloon. A considerable stretch of time must have passed. Jim the Penitent Brother-in-Law had flogged two livid red circles into his back.

I idled by the entrance of the tent. The one-man band walked by, playing an accidental tune. People were leaving the tent, crossing the grass and the dirt street, heading into the dark. In their transit they huddled close to each other, and from them came an air of tired giddiness, and a bit of fear, just as you'd find at a carnival closing for the night. Jim had stopped whipping his back. He rolled his hood up over his nose and began eating a skewer of eel. He had several of them in the same hand as his scourge. He'd bought them at a discount as the vendor packed up for the night, or so I reasoned.

I went inside the tent, and indeed most of the congregation had gone, but there remained a third and final preacher. She was an old woman. She stood on the trampled grass, under a fearsome limelight, encircled by her audience. She wore a black bonnet and a black dress, a fashion between a nurse and a Mennonite. Beneath the caustic glare of the burning limelight, her face and hands were pale blue. Her eyes were shining and dark and they released tears. The whole of her quivered.

I couldn't make out a word, but when she spoke, her mouth moved like a black flame. She paused, licking her lips. One heard the rasp of it. One heard the lime burning. Such was the quiet she inspired.

She looked at me. True, I was the tallest man in a sparse crowd. But her gaze was odd, both sudden and gentle, as though we knew each other.

Martens tugged at my sleeve.

For some reason, his hair caught my eye. It was at odds with his face. In the cast of the limelight, his hair was glossy and black. Black to the point of blue. But then the stubble across his chin, for he had not shaven, was pure white. Did Martens dye his hair?

Had I been wrong about him? Had this primeval man retained some vanity?

He pulled my arm. I followed.

Outside, Jim was gone. The little goblinesque man was at the saloon door, sticking his head in and shouting in French, "You're slaves! Slaves all!"

Martens was tramping away fast. He called to me over his shoulder, "Nowak, did the Holy Ghost visit you?"

"No, sir," I said.

"No?" he said, his voice wavering. "But the Spirit was manifest."

"Right, sir," I said. "I saw everyone shaking."

"Shaking," he said, a weak echo. "You had only to open yourself, Nowak, to know your own soul."

"I see, sir. Did the Holy Ghost visit you, Mister Martens?" I said.

"It did," he shouted from somewhere ahead.

"Did you shake?"

"I did not shake, Nowak," he called back. "The Holy Ghost shook *me*."

"I see, sir."

"You see nothing, Nowak!" he said, suddenly angry. We had walked into the dark, into what seemed the yet further outskirts of Philadelphia. He stopped and turned on me. The night was moonless. I could not see, but I felt his anger tunnel through the black air. I feared he would chuck a rock at my head. "Nowak, do you not know your own soul?"

"In honesty, Mister Martens," I said, "I don't understand what you mean."

"What are you?"

"Sir?"

"Are you a Jew? A Mohammedan? A heathen?"

"I was raised in the Holy Roman Church," I said.

I had no idea what he was after or why.

"Have you never looked within," he said, "and there beheld the gift of God?"

"No, sir," I said.

"Because you refuse!" he said, and after his voice died further out in the dark, he spat, and then cried out, "*I* know my soul! *I* am a follower of the light!"

With that, he tramped off again.

There was not a house in sight. We were crossing long squares of grass and mud where the beginning of streets had been cut in the earth. "Sir," I called after him, "are we heading the right way?"

Later in the dark, I called again, "Mister Martens?"

He gave no reply.

Further into the dark, I asked, "Mister Martens! Are you following the light back to the ship?"

"Go to Hell, Nowak!" he shouted from a field ahead of me. "To Hell!" he shouted. "You squander God's gift!"

I don't know where he went, but I was soon alone. The earth inclined, quickening my steps, and I perceived that I was skirting a hill, a gentle hill it seemed, save near its top where it became a severe, blocky plateau, a solid shape in the murk. I made distance from the sudden thing, and it formed turrets against the sky. It was a titanic structure. In a few months, I would know it as a prison.

NINE

On return to Danzig, I was twenty or twenty-one. I had seen the world, or Philadelphia anyway. Danzig, in comparison, seemed serene and healthsome, all stone and sun-caught panes of glass. Even the bustle on the quay was blessedly calm. Philadelphia, I thought, was a lunatic child with a blade in hand.

I knew, in some way, I was fated to call it home.

These thoughts came to me within the confines of the Meteorite.

On the first and second day back in Danzig, I stayed aboard. My eyes were never far from our gangplank. I hoped and prayed that Klara would appear at our slip on the quayside as Captain Langobard, a man of experience, had predicted.

But on the third day, I woke in a panic, wondering whether I had misunderstood Klara. She had ordered me to stay away from the tavern. But perhaps it was a test. Did she want me to defy her? I brushed down my sailor's uniform, shined my boots, weighed down my curls with a palmful of hair oil and set out to find her.

Better to burn my bed than lie in doubt.

I had never been to her tavern in daylight. First, there was a sign I'd never noticed. "Glockner's," it said. The steps down were wide and familiar. To my surprise, the whole of the tavern was rather more posh than I realized. Napkins lay at each table setting.

With it near empty at midday, the odd fit of the space was apparent. The bar, for instance, was tucked around to the side, short in length and obscured by pillars. Two gentlemen leaned there, talking in a friendly rumble to the tender. The tender, a small and bald man with a towel over his shoulder, looked to me and said, "Hallo, young fellow. What can I get you?"

I asked whether Miss Klara was available. The gentlemen looked over their shoulders and took my measure.

"Miss Klara's not well, I'm afraid," said the tender, "but I'm her husband, the proprietor."

This was Louis Glockner, naturally. 'Til then, I had no notion of his existence. After a few moments, as I failed to respond, he asked: "Are you the new kegman she told me about?"

"Yes," I said, "I'm the kegman," and, taking my leave, I added, "One moment, please."

Once outside, I moved as if pursued. The sky was pale blue. That square off Hintergasse listed like a ship on heavy swells. I came into Longmarket. Everyone was strolling, gazing. I barreled through and came to rest finally on a barstool in another saloon. I stared into the sweating metal neck of a beer tap. The droplets blazed with great intensity, loaded with sunlight.

"Look alive, boy!" said the barman, an old salt. I had been there many times before. He slid me a beer. It, too, was full of the Sun. I drank it down and got to business, transacting only with the barman. The drinks dulled my nerves, yet my senses grew keener, at least in the realm of thought.

Of course Klara was married. She was a beautiful and fully grown woman. Hell, by age she could be my mother! She probably was *someone's* mother, I reasoned. And of course I was not her first dalliance. Recall the prowess, nay, the tranquility with which she took me to bed. One strong look from her, and any man would falter. What a fool, what a fool I had been!

I settled with the barman. I had outpaced him, and I walked out into the night three or four drinks ahead of the game. The city was slick with an errant rainfall. I staggered back to the Meteorite.

Learning that Klara was married was a dreadful blow. In fact, no psychic pain had ever registered so acutely in my body. My muscles ached. My head swam. A searing pain tore my chest. But I lost no more than a few days to it. Three? I can't be sure. Either way, one morning my feet hit the cold wood deck of the crew's cabin and I reckoned that my life, in essence, was unchanged.

I reported for duty.

Mister Reich had us hands carry aboard the last of the provisions, and at noon, rather than lose us for the day, he ordered us to tar the ropes. Men climbed the rigging with pails and brushes while others, such as myself, stayed below with rags and knives to clean up the fallen globs of tar. Too many of us were on the task. Buffoonery ensued. Men wrestled. Up in the ropes, they chased each other. I watched the people on the quayside, the stewards, agents, sailors, dockers, hawkers and valets, the passengers and passersby. They shouted, cried and laughed, or slipped soundlessly around each other. Silence gathered over me, and a hot trickle played upon my scalp.

Someone snorted.

The snort came from a sailor named Wolkwitz. He was hanging upside down in the ropes with a bright grin across his face. From his brush he had dribbled tar into my hair. A thread of the black stuff fell across my forehead. Laughter broke out from the rigging and across the deck. I went under to clean off the goop.

In the crew lavatory, I managed to scrub the stuff from my skin. My hair was a lost cause. With shears I cut it down to the scalp and flushed the curls down the toilet and into the river.

At the gulp of the pipe, I felt again the loss of Klara. Over the last weeks I had nurtured a vision, a sort of waking dream: Klara and Józef with a home, an attic apartment in Danzig, or in Philadelphia, morning glories on the window sill. The sound of children's footfalls. I saw myself by those flowers, waiting for the children. I was a good man. A husband, a father. But this vision disappeared, and my heart fled my body to run after it, searching the streets and hills, like a dog chasing echoes of its master's call. Those of its true master. Not me. Oh, my thoughts! They were half-things with jagged edges. Broken cups. The toilet burped again and swallowed the last of my hair. I checked the mirror. There I was.

The monks had always cut the hair of us Józefs down to the scalp.

I tied a rag around my head and went topside to rejoin the work. The men dangled in the rigging and huddled by the masts. At my return, a cry went up. "He's back!" they shouted. "Nice headdress, Nowak!"

Embarrassed, I pulled the rag from my head.

The howls redoubled.

My name henceforth was Baby Fuzz.

That evening Langobard brought the crew around a pig roast. The cooks improvised a fire in a box of bricks on the foredeck and cooked the meat according to some tropical tradition involving fruit. The flavor of it cut the ranting of the crew down to a happy whisper. We ate cross legged against the gunwale and rolled bottles of liquor back and forth to each other over the rivets.

I was despondent.

"Baby Fuzz is in love with a whore," one sailor explained to another.

"Is that right?" said the other to me, wiping his mouth on his sleeve.

I hadn't the energy to respond.

"They're cunning whores in Danzig," said Muller, a senior seaman. Pig fat shone across lips and hands. "I'm sure she's a lovely gal besides," he said.

"Now he wants to marry her," said the first, meat falling from his mouth.

"Why's that?" said the other.

"Because I love her!" I said. Admittedly, I'd had my share of the bottles.

"But she's already married," the first sailor explained to the other.

Muller clamped a greasy hand on my shoulder. "Every man gets stabbed in the heart," he said, and he thereupon began the tale of his own romantic woe, and as he spoke, various versions of my humiliation spread around the deck, and before Muller had reached the climax of his tale, all the young hands like me had strolled up, pig meat pursed in their fingers. "C'mon, Baby Fuzz," they said.

"Come with us."

The fellows treated me to a few drinks at a beer hall, but I soon escaped into the quiet nighttime streets and returned to the Meteorite. I climbed into my bunk and slept. Sometime later, the curtain of my bunk parted, and a woman came into my bed.

A cold mouth opened upon my lips, and small, hard hands tugged on the waist of my trousers. I came roaring out of sleep with my lust at a boiling pitch. I crushed this woman to me, spanning the whole of her spiny back with my hands.

Here was my thought: this creature is too small, too insubstantial to be Klara.

Her mouth tightened on mine.

An instant later, I was outside of my bed. I had leapt out, shoving the woman aside. The air had the smell of dark earth and sea. I stood in the crew's quarters, between the walls of bunks. From behind the berth curtains came grunts, moans, laughter and rhythmic slapping. The young sailors had returned from drinking with a brothel's worth of whores in tow. I found myself face-to-face with Kaulitz, a friendly apprentice seaman with a patchy beard. He was staring out from his bunk, "Baby Fuzz," he said, "have you seen my girl?"

The woman that had woken me emerged from behind the curtain of my bunk.

"I beg your pardon, miss," I said.

She crawled in with Kaulitz.

"Where have you been?" he demanded.

"There's too many of you," she hissed back.

"C'mon, c'mon," he said, drawing the curtain.

I stood a moment longer in the sound and odor of the shrouded whore-mongering. Want struck me in the heart. No one but Klara would do. I went back to Glockner's.

Before long on that night, I stood in the midst of the tables of Glockner's tavern and called Klara's name. She did not recognize me. Not at first. Over eight weeks had passed since we had last seen one another, sixty-some days since we had disrobed in the darkness of Kotlowitz & Sons, and here I was without a coat, shorn of hair and spattered with tar.

In a sense, I did not recognize her. How else to describe the way she outstripped my senses? Even my longing had underplayed her. Klara was brighter and darker, yet more a miracle than I had remembered. Summer had started, and she must have taken in the Sun, tinting her skin and unearthing the copper in her black hair, or else it was a trick of the colors she wore. A green scarf to tie up her hair, a yellow blouse open at the neck. Her black eyes shone—I had startled her, of course.

I took her by the wrist. "I don't care that you're married," I said.

"Get out," she said. "I can't—"

"Or whether you have children. I want to marry you. To be your —"

Klara yanked her wrist from my hand.

There was trouble. The feet of barstools rubbed on the floor. I had touched the barmaid, and several men had stood from their tables. I sensed them behind and to the side of me. I'll be all right, I thought, yet staring at Klara. I can take a beating.

Klara waved the men off and pushed me down into a seat at an empty table. For several minutes thereafter she ignored me. It was anguish.

She brought men their drinks, she collected

their coins and bills and wiped down the tables. She nodded to Louis, who stood behind the bar, and told him that nothing was wrong.

Klara returned to me, bringing a stein down with such force that a drop of foam shot straight up in the air. "You cannot be here," she said. "Drink this and go."

"I haven't any money," I said.

"It's on the house," she said.

I then whispered to her in dialect, Kashubian, or my best guess at it: "I am for you. You are for me."

Looking back, I suppose I ought to disavow this conduct.

Klara's eyes flared with a bright and whole fury, or fear. I felt the charge of it in my chest, as though my lungs were under her command.

"Drink and get out of here," she said, adding a vulgar oath.

With that she returned to her duties, her life. The men at the tables all around were eyeing me over their drinks.

For a long while, I held my head in my hands. On some vague principle, I refused to drink the beer. Its foam thinned and the glass shed its moisture into a puddle on the table. I wasn't drunk, not enough for any action. In fact, a ray of awful sobriety cleaved my head. More men came into the bar. They lit pipes, raised up the chatter and sang.

Klara passed in her orbits. With my eyes closed, I traced her passings by the sound of her heels on the stone and the clink and thud of the steins she set down and collected. She took the beer from me. I opened my eyes. There in the puddle lay a note that read:

In heaven they take not in marriage—Matthew 22

I stared at those words, at the ink blearing in beer and water. For a moment, my spirit tumbled like a feather. I smashed my fist down upon the table and cried, "Horseshit!"

My reaction surprised me, and Klara. She was a few steps away, clearing glasses from a table. One fell, but only clanked against the floor.

However, a man to my left was not surprised. He'd been waiting, coiled, and he jumped up and knocked me clean from my stool with a single strike on the jaw.

For a while, I lay on the floor and beheld the vaulted ceiling. Then I got to my feet. The man who struck me had his knuckles up, and I could tell by his widening eyes that he hadn't fathomed me for such a tall fellow.

I righted my stool, intending to sit, but a feeling stopped me. Better to leave, it said.

You've made your point. Enough humiliation for one night.

How strange, this feeling, a species of restraint.

I left the cellar bar. I climbed the stairs, one foot after another. Perhaps I had lost some boyish illusions. Clarity's a poor comfort. Out I rose from the tobacco smoke and into the dispiriting chill of the night.

[Second Folio—Damaged]

Ten

When I left, I intended the exit to be final.
[*Text destroyed* ...]
I won't expound on my pain and self-loathing,
[...]
my soul is clothed in a hair shirt.
[...]
a cat yowling from atop a dark wall, the crash of an unseen door,
[...]
the circuit of stone lanes
[...]
Terror and understanding work in odd order.

[*Klara meets Martens on the quayside. They remember one another* ...]

"A heart, sister?"
"A heart in the sky," said Klara to the carpenter.
[...]
"Oh," Martens cried, "the way of the Lord, it is so hard to know. It is obscure!
[...]
just as the air is obscure to our lungs," he said, "yet we breathe!"
[...]

I kneel before you once again," he said. "The world gives no quarter until we submit to His will."

[...]

so much vein and bone. An appearance of life and death at once.

[...]

a man at God's gate, crying to be let in.

[...]

Nowak!" Martens cried. "He is like you!"

[...]

To the east, towards the Vistula River, towards Konigsberg and Russia, the sky was turning purple. Gulls flew, tilting their white bodies. Dawn was coming. Wagons would clatter on streets. Starlings in trees were already waking. There was a mist upon the river. The ships would soon take to the sea.

TWELVE

[*Klara takes passage on The Meteorite. She falls ill and meets Kindersley, the ship's nurse and friend to Martens ...*]

When Klara regained herself, she was lying on a cot in a white room. She sat up. Nearby, a familiar image hung on the wall: Saint Michael the Archangel, the icon. This icon was silver plated, and so Michael shone, wings spread and sword drawn. His hair was painted gold. He pinned the head of a heretic underfoot.

[...]

The old woman was at the sink. She worked a foot pedal. Water came from the faucet in a bright stream. She washed her hands.

This was Nurse Kindersley.

[...]

the whole of her was apiece with the light—white hair and skin, dress and cap—as though she were the memory of a body.

[...]

"Who do you think I am?" Klara said.

"You're the Woman of the Wild. Or you may be, if we follow His will," the nurse said, glancing at the ceiling and, presumably, Heaven.

[...]

She turned on the stool and opened a cabinet lined with jars. She took from it a mug covered with a saucer. Handing the mug to Klara, she said, "I've kept this for you. Coffee to set you right. Lots of sugar."

[...]

The nurse returned to the cabinet and retrieved one of the jars from the bottom row. She held it close before Klara. It read, *Arsenic*.

The nurse unscrewed its lid.

"For the rats, dear," she said. She stood and moved around the little room, and as she did, she sprinkled a path of white powder around its edge.

[...]

said Nurse Kindersley, "I know your man Nowak. And I'm glad you've brought him up. Lift your legs, dear." The nurse bent and bobbed low, walking as would a crab. She shook out arsenic beneath the bed. The little room now smelled of garlic and powdered sugar. Klara covered her mouth.

"You see," the nurse said, "there's no Man of the Wild."

"Pardon?"

"In scripture, dear," the nurse said, straightening up and screwing on the jar's lid. "In God's truth as revealed, Revelation, Chapter 12, one through seventeen, there's the woman, the child, and the woman alone. She has no man."

[Klara journeys on The Meteorite out of the Baltic and North Seas ...]

[...]

then came the Irish.

[...]

the island's sons and daughters.

[...]

choir of a thousand strains

[...]

a darkly clad wave, up the gangway

[...]

peasants freed from the yoke of the land.

[...]

rail to rail, they'd overwhelm little the spaces around the funnels and aft mast and lifeboats and capstans and piles of their own belongings

[...]

The first meal, which commenced just after losing sight of Dublin city, was pea soup and rye bread and green tea, served in a tin pail with utensils and a tin cup. This kit was given once and never again. Without it, the steerage goer cannot eat. Klara got the kit from a queue that snaked from the mess into the steerage cabin. She escaped the crowded cabin and ate in the open air. The food wasn't good, but not so awful that you'd chuck it into the wake. Yet half the passengers did. Half again then complained of their hunger.

Witness how sea travel makes madness!

The heat of the summer let in a wind from the north and put a mean chop in the sea, causing the Meteorite to shake. The Sun lowered toward the far side of Ireland.

[...]

How the sea unleashes man's lust!

Gone are all containments. The forest and hills, the bricks, courts, and constables, all certainties, past and future

[...]

she sat in a little mob of passengers along the starboard gunwale

[...]

a hand came to the back of her skirts and passed around to touch her bosom. The man breathed into her hair and pressed her leg. His credentials hardened through his pants.

[...]

The supper that evening was white beans with spare flecks of grey pork, hard biscuit and black tea. Much of it again got chucked into the Irish Sea.

[...]

Later, stars hung overhead, as if arrested in their fall. A man sawed at a fiddle and another strummed a guitar. A small crowd of men and women—boys and girls really—griped at them, "Get on with it!" The boys and girls shoved each other, curtsied and bowed, and took each other by the hand to dance. The girls gave the boys looks. They gripped the boys by the shoulders. They kicked at their feet. The boys, those with the mettle, reeled the girls around. Someone passed Klara a clay jug. It was cold and unstoppered. She gulped from it, and the sting of gin went right to the back of her head. A man took her and reeled her around. Klara got her bearing and pulled away. The man that spun her now sat beside her. The wool of his jacket smelled like smoke. Nearby, a girl stabbed a boy's thigh with a hat pin. His friend pulled it out. The party went on, that is until the stewards intervened at curfew. The girls hung still for a moment, then flew to the dark end of the deck.

They were as radiant as blackbirds. They shouted, calling the stewards what must have been vulgar names. The boys whistled and cheered.

At length, the stewards wrangled them all indoors.

[...]

The ladies commiserated in their varieties of expression, laughing, talking of the men and the food and the noise and the lack of air around the berths and in the lavatory and the sickening, slow tilt of the ship and more.

[...]

It was never really quiet. Someone was always rustling, snoring, sneezing or coughing, or whispering to another, and from beyond the tacked sheet came the cries of small children and shushes of their parents.

[...]

Dawn came as a grey glow.

[...]

Eyes flashed through the dim space.

[...]

The sky was yet a starry pitch that fell behind the horizon. Until at once

[...]

the Sun, a fiery line cracking the sea, reaching across the waves.

[...]

from the deck above, a sailor was watching her.

[...]

navy short jacket snug to his shoulders and arms, and the wide legged pants were trim to his thighs. His hair was gold, his skin bronze. But troubling his beauty was his manner. He held the railing. His eyes were wide. Watching Klara, the beautiful sailor was afraid, or in awe.

This was Mikkal Persson.

I have delayed introducing Persson. He hasn't yet had a hand in the events, but more to the point, I despise him. Even now that he's dead, on writing his name a seed of disgust breaks open within me.

Persson was a rich man's son, an heir to a controlling interest in the Dutch and Danish firm that owned the Meteorite. At port, he'd stride the deck stripped to waist, showing off a classical musculature. Persson had no job on the ship, but would work at his whim. He did all with ease, often complex tasks of derring-do in the rigging.

From the first sight of him, my throat turned hot. I kept a distance.

But the man had a face that was hard not to look at. It was symmetrical, of perfect proportion, and smooth, as though by God's intent. His eyes were unnaturally bright, blue or green, and had an Asiatic tilt (the gift of a Saami forebear?). His size, however, made him appear strange.

He was small. Small such that one had to glance twice to gauge him against his surroundings, say within a doorway or beside a table.

THIRTEEN

Apropos of nothing, and all at once, I hated the sea.

It's absurd, of course, to hate the sea, but I did. I hated it as I'd hated nothing before. In fact, I'm not sure I had truly hated anything until that moment when I hated the sea, its tiresome grandeur, flat and dazzling. On it goes in stupid infinity.

And the sky, always so bright, even at night. That was another kind of horror.

[...]

Good Lord! The galling monotony!

[...]

I had gone to sea for adventure, but against the sea all adventure is imbecilic.

[...]

days like sips of poison.

[...]

wound up and was black in my moods

[...]

duties slip

[...]

Dudko, the chief stoker, had no pity. Here was a man poisoned through.

One night, somewhere at the start of the Atlantic, he cuffed me on the ear for arriving late. I turned on him and snapped the handle of a shovel over my knee.

He backed out of the fireroom, becoming two white eyes in the black passageway.

Later, at breaktime, no one came. I endured a few hours and then stepped to the empty passageway, but a fear kept me from calling out for relief. Dudko was still in the passageway, watching me. I sensed it.

For nights thereafter, I would shovel without break or water.

One morning I tottered my way to the boatswain's office, Mister Reich's tiny chamber. I had a mind to complain of Dudko, that his revenge was too cruel, but the heat had demolished my senses.

I babbled at Reich, gnashing my teeth and shedding tears.

"Baby Fuzz," said Reich, "did you read the terms of your work contract? Do you realize that you're on the hook for the cost of passage across the sea over the life of the contract? Do you understand me?"

I did not.

"That's food, berth and ticket, Baby Fuzz. Three

years worth. Now, if we must do away with your labor because you've breached terms of contract, say by disobeyance or malingering, as you've just implied, you remain on the hook for that cost, only you've lost your wage to pay it —".

"Sir," I said, breaking into my right mind, "you mean to say that by working this ship I owe you money?"

"Not me, Fuzz," said Reich, looking less a gnome and more a man, "you owe the venture, the company, yes. As of this moment you owe —" Reich paused, and after some moments of figuring in his head, he spoke a number that hit me like a cold wave.

I let out something of a bark.

Then, back in my cramped and stinking berth, for which I was paying handsomely, again I could not sleep.

[...]

The book was in English, but I'd made headway through a few dozen pages. The title was *Dash Andrews, Installment 4, The weird narrative of a lost man.*

The dime novel stoked within me dreams of the American West, that land of myth, its deserts and mountains and forests, its plains replete with buffalo, desperados, lawmen, snakes, Indians, eagles, cowboys, and antelope

[...]

I'll spare you the meaningless details of my dream. Suffice it to say that I was walking in the desert. There was a train.

[...]

My shift began

[...]

a thump on the fireroom door.

[...]

We fought in the passageway. A blow crashed

[...]

As Dudko advanced, a man with iron hands grabbed me from behind. So there were two. Dudko and another. Of this, I am certain.

[...]

The second man pulled me back into the fireroom.

[...]

Dudko, the fiend, meant to kill me. My hands clinched his throat, I lifted him up, and we crashed and rolled in the coal. I kept my purchase around his neck, his neck hardened, and his white eyes goggled out from the dark plain of his face. I wanted only to survive. A stench came up between us. A dark and wet smell, like shit, but also like a forest in spring.

[...]

From behind, the iron hands of the second man, a man unseen, lifted me

[...]

I saw stars, and Dudko slipped away.

Blood poured off of my elbow.

I hadn't seen the knife, and a long moment occurred, a moment in which I stared at the cut and blade. Dudko had driven a knife into the jointure of my left arm.

Surrounded by fire and smoke

[...]

gnawing sensation spread as though bilge rats had arrived and had begun to eat

[...]

My mind was clear. I did not feel the presence of God.

FOURTEEN

As it happens, I did not die. There was a surgeon traveling on the Meteorite, and even before the fire was out, he was there with his kit.

This surgeon knelt by me, passed his lantern to a hand—Kaulitz, again—and fastened a tourniquet, a canvas strap with a buckle, below my shoulder. He pressed his fingers into the wound, feeling for the source of the blood's spurt, and found by the lantern's light that the blade had cut an artery. It was a mere nick. The surgeon handed Kaulitz a length of tube and ordered him to suck away the blood. Kaulitz, bless him, stuck the tube's end in the wound and sucked 'til my blood kissed his lips. Meanwhile the surgeon pinched off the artery with two pairs of small, silver forceps, clamping them on either side of the nick. But blood continued to fill the wound. To find the second source, the surgeon took a scalpel in hand and sliced upward into the tissue of my arm.

He dug around in the muscle and realized that another artery had been cut. This one right through. Worse, each severed end of the artery had retreated from the insult of Dudko's blade, such that one end now hid in my forearm, and the other had snapped back within the meat of my bicep. The surgeon cut deep in both directions and retrieved these ends. He clamped them closed and began to sew. He sewed shut the nick on the first artery. Crouching close, ordering Kaulitz to hold the lantern by his eyes, he then sewed together the soft wet circles of the severed artery. A delicate, slippery task. Once done, he unbuckled the tourniquet, watched the wound for a minute or more, then stitched shut the whole affair.

The surgeon, soaked in blood and seawater, did it all in a quarter of an hour. The fire was out. Captain Langobard and several of the crew stood over him, admiring the man's work.

The surgeon's name was Jakub Davidson.

I recall my first conversation with him, a conversation into which my awareness arrived like a train screaming to a halt. I found myself in the white space of sickbay. Davidson was at my bedside.

He was a man with a cloud of hair and sparkling, round spectacles.

With morphine, he had softened the grinding gears of my pain. He ministered doses to himself, as well. We were both weeping, baring our souls.

He was Jewish, he told me, born in Danzig, the son of a wealthy timber merchant. As a boy he traveled with his father down the Vistula and into Poland's forested innards. There were black horses pulling skids and lumberjacks eating apples beneath the leaves. At eighteen, he stole money, beat it to Warsaw and was admitted into the Academy of Fine Arts. When Jakub returned to Danzig, his father commended the young man's work canvas-by-canvas, but by principle tossed each into the fire. A compromise was struck. Jakub would become a doctor, but would do so where he pleased. Before the year was out, Jakub was in America, Philadelphia, studying anatomy at the University of Pennsylvania. When the so-called Southern Confederacy took up its treason, Davidson served the Union as a surgeon. For four years he stood in blood and cut limbs. When peace came, Davidson left the army with a stubborn habit for morphine, the gold oak leaf of a major, and a vow to never again cut human flesh and bone. (A vow he broke on me). Having abandoned the scalpel, he pursued a career as a medical lecturer at his alma mater. He persisted as a Jew among gentiles, a bachelor, a dopehead and melancholiac.

One afternoon, after a heavy dose, Davidson awoke on the floor of his university office to Robert Alvin Summers, a colleague and fellow medical lecturer, slapping him about the face. Summers had been a major and a battlefield surgeon as well, though for the South. He was a loud man, a family man, a father of eight. His cheeks were always crimson. His hands rested in fists. On a day soon after Summers' rescue of Davidson from the overdose, he took the sad doctor on a train to Boston. There, Summers had an appointment with an elderly woman that claimed to be magnetic.

Summers and Davidson sat in her kitchen. She picked up a spoon with the back of her hand. She waved her arm about, but the spoon remained affixed across her knuckles.

After that, Davidson went with Summers to an Ohio farm to meet a man that glowed green in the dark. They tested him in the root cellar, then in the barn at night, and even beneath a dining room table covered with heavy blankets. The Ohioan's glow would not dim.

Davidson, by his lonesome, then spent the autumn with vampire hunters in the woods of Maine.

He and Summers soon published *Apparition and Reality*, a seminal text on the supernatural, after which Davidson embarked on *Views of the Soul*.

In *Views of the Soul*, Davidson examines persons of all manner—class, race, religious affiliation— that happen to share a peculiar experience:

At night and very occasionally in the day, these people have entered trances wherein they see as God might see: it begins with God's eye, a large eye, luminous and black.

Secondary phenomena occur: floating, extreme cold, accounts of strange behavior from deer, spiders, cats and other creatures. But the eye of God awaits above them, if occasionally interpreted as the eyes of angels or some entity yet unknown.

After meeting the eye, the experiencer sees into it, and then sees as though possessing the eye. They see the Earth from the heavens. They observe the faces and hands of loved ones and strangers. Their sight barrels between the heights. Sparrows fall, and the very hairs of your head are numbered, etcetera, as per the Word of God.

Klara may have been such a seer. Or so says Davidson's notes. She appears in them as "Marya." I found her in his papers in 1885, about four years after the main events of this narrative, when Doctor Robert Alvin Summers and I were sifting through the materials of Davidson's study in Philadelphia. Together Summers and I completed *Views of the Soul* for publication in winter 1888. The scant account of Klara, or Marya, which was Davidson's last case, didn't make it into the text. In his surviving notes, she's little more than a captured phrase. "A heart in the sky," wrote Davidson's hand, after which he added "Desert—Spirit—pregnant," and "Józef."

Anything else he wrote of her, and me, was lost.

Of other subjects, Davidson had pages upon pages. He always began with an interview, asking the subject whether they had taken part in the Occult, Theosophy, Necromancy, Mesmerism, Palm Reading, Séances, or Psychometry, whether they had experimented with Ouija Tables, Spiritoscopes, or Exploring Pendulums, and whether they were aware of Body Atmospheres, Od Rays, or Soul Odors, all of which Davidson considered bunk, but would explore so as to disentangle from genuine phenomena. He would then perform an eye exam, and ask whether they had ever hallucinated for hunger, for lack of sleep, or for extreme heat or cold, or whether they had ever suffered a strong blow to the head. After sounding these depths, Davidson would begin hypnosis—a methodological step he regretted, but found indispensable—and once they fell under he would probe their hidden memory, recording the content of what was seen through the eye of God.

On one afternoon in 1880 while in the weeds of these testimonies, Davidson was piecing together the glimpses and shreds when he received a telegram from his sister in Danzig. She asked him to return and mediate a conflict between their brothers. The Davidson timber fortune was at stake. As Jakub packed a trunk, he included his long unused surgeon's kit, as though to show his family that he had kept his end of the bargain. He sailed from Philadelphia.

From where the ship docked in Danzig, it was a short walk down the Longmarket to the family home. There he sat at a desk with several ledgers by the light of a window that was shut to the market's clatter of wheels on cobblestone and the screeching of gulls and the smoke that travels in Danzig's air. The ledgers' columns produced in him a sensation of suffocation, of heat pressing through one's face and neck, of being eradicated. He looked up at his sister and two brothers.

"Well?" they asked.

They were strangers to him, repositories of their dead parents, this business, this house, these ledgers and the light, water and chill of Danzig. He, of course, was likewise a stranger to them.

"I would sell everything," Jakub replied.

He stayed for a few nights and boarded a ship back to Philadelphia.

Somewhere past Ireland, as I have already related, he saved my life.

My wound became infected, gangrenous. Fever closed down my conversations with Doctor Davidson, and I was cognizant but once more before we landed in Philadelphia:

Captain Langobard materialized in the daylight.

"Look sharp, Nowak," he said.

Langobard was peering close. His head stayed in place, but his body revolved as though it were the hands of a clock. "You in there, Nowak? Eh? Say something."

"Yessir," I managed.

"Yes, well, all right then," Langobard said. "Enjoying a lie-in, are we?"

Reich appeared at the blurry edge of things.

"Sign here, Mister Nowak," said Reich. He lifted my hand and closed my fingers around a pen.

"No shirking, Nowak," said Langobard. "Sign the bloody thing."

A sheet of paper hovered before me, and beneath a block of letters, I made some manner of a line.

"Is this my contract for the next leg, sir?" I heard myself say.

"Don't be daft, Nowak," said Langobard. "It's your confession. You're going to hang for what you've done. Arson, assault! Poor Dudko, the man can no longer talk!"

"Sir," I said, "there were two men, sir. Dudko

and another."

Langobard's face, still at the center of the dial, folded in confusion.

"A second man?" said Reich. He was yet in the blur of my periphery. "Did you get a look at him, Nowak?"

"No sir, Mister Reich," I said. "He pulled me from behind as Mister Dudko —"

"Don't tell tales, Nowak!" roared Langobard. The captain was at once drifting at a great distance and right within my skull. "Mister Reich, let us not confuse matters further," said Langobard. "This bloody oaf may well have cost us our jobs."

"I'm sorry, sir," I said.

"Shut up, Nowak," said Langobard. "We have your confession, sworn depositions from the victim, and my writ of fact, which is equal to any governor's. You're done for, Nowak. Done for. Now, avail yourself to Yahweh, or Adonai, or whatever you Jews call Him. Which is it, Reich?"

Reich, in the mist, said, "Adonai will do, Captain."

"Very good," said Langobard, and with that he and Reich receded into the daylight and became thin black marks. The door opened and in rushed the scentless air of the sea.

"And, Nowak," Langobard called, "do cooperate

with the good doctor here. He's a guest, a paying passenger, and is doing that arm of yours a rather large favor."

The sight of my arm preceded my sensation of it. It had swollen, stretching the skin to the burnished sheen of a roasted pig. Here and there purple mounds pushed up. They looked like plums. The smell of the wound was foul, and the feeling of it all was so bizarre that I hesitate to call it pain. It was as though my arm had turned to stone, crushing the bones within, but the sensation was not in the arm itself. Inexplicably, the crush registered in my eyes and teeth.

Doctor Davidson, whom for the moment I could not recall having seen before, was washing his hands at the sink and muttering an order to Nurse Kindersley, whom I saw then for the first time. She seemed to me made of paper. She covered my nose with a rag of chloroform or ether, some cold fume with a sharp tip that spiraled upward into my head. A certain darkness vibrated around me.

"Bite this,'" she said. By then, I could no longer feel my mouth. She had snuffed me out.

Davidson had resolved to cut off the spoiled limb. He worked fast, once again summoning his battlefield skill. He cut high up on my bicep. He tied off the arteries with silk thread, then sawed through the bone and filed it smooth. He sliced a squared-off cape from the remaining muscle and skin, which he then folded over and sewed shut, save for a small slit from where the wound could drain. Having removed the bulk of my left arm, he wrapped it in a bed sheet and a few minutes later stepped onto the main deck and handed it to a steward with instructions that it burn in the furnace.

The steward made it halfway down the deck when, in revulsion, he threw my arm overboard into the water.

It would have floated, no? The rocking of the waves would loosen it from the sheet. My left arm, which was red and purple at its separation from me, would turn white and green and swell yet larger, both with seawater and its own putrescent gas. Sharks might take flinching bites, smaller fish would peck, stripping it down and allowing its descent. I see the bones aglow in the murk.

It was once a boy's unblemished limb. Soft and thin. Later, freckles and golden white hair appeared. It lengthened, matured. Deltas of blue veins emerged in the wrist, the forearm muscle, and the back of its hand.

It bore two scars: one moon-shaped from a

mean monk and a fire poker, and the other a cross of white tissue: spider bite, lanced.

My dear left could catch, but it could not throw. In the project of walking, it balanced the swing of my right. My left aimed my rifle for Polish freedom, though my right had little cause to pull the trigger. That night in Kotlowitz & Sons, my left ran its hand through Klara's long hair.

That hand caressed her back, intuiting the bone and muscle, feeling the softness, skin and sweat.

At rest, when I read books, it held the pages I had passed. When I wrote, it would cup my cheek and chin and steady the paper with its elbow.

Now as I write so many years later—weighing down the paper with the lonely heel of my right hand—I am yet unable to accept that my left arm is gone. On occasion, I'll reach for a doorknob with the scarred, slim stump that remains. My stump gestures when I speak, and I witness the flicker of disgust in others as it moves within my pinned up sleeve. Mirrors shock me. My asymmetry appears a mistake of angle or lighting. My partialness a trick of the eye. I fall into trances. I am at discord with existence. I cannot accept its absence. Pain comes stalking as I lay in bed. My dream mind opens. Its ghost itches. It throbs. And when the night is especially cruel, bolts of lightning rebound to the fingers that are not there.

Stranger yet, in broad daylight, is the urge to chew on my stump.

My jaw tightens, wishing to cut the scarred vestige between its teeth. I admit, I have succumbed. I have broken its skin. A sign of insanity.

Forgive me, I say to what remains. *Don't leave me.*

The stump, so sweet a creature, it cheers me, as though saying, *Someday the rest of us will return.* My prodigal arm will have aged in its travels. Sharper knuckles. Deeper creases. Its skin will be a patchwork of brown.

I still dream of being whole.

I came out of the anesthesia as though I were condensing from a cloud. First came my throat, so dry, and then my jaw, followed by my eyes and, far down below, my toes. Doctor Davidson was standing above me. Apparently we had been talking.

"It's all right, my boy," said Davidson. "You're more than a strong back and pair of hands, you know. God gave you a heart and mind, as well," he said. "Now you must put them to the service of your fellow man!"

That doctor. He had the look of a stage comedian

at rest. A broad white mustache over a gap-toothed smile. Wiry hair half-tamed. Twinkling blue-grey eyes behind crooked spectacles. At once, his air of friendly sadness absorbed me.

I recall weeping.

"Listen," said the doctor, "you must keep it clean. Ask your jailers for the following: *iodine*."

"*Iodine*," I repeated, mimicking his English.

"Good. Also, *bandages*."

"*Bandages*."

"It will take about two months to heal, my boy. Change the dressing when you can, and above all, keep the wound clean."

I wept again. The anesthetic had overrun me with love and delirium. "Thank you, doctor!" I cried, my throat thick with tears. "You're a wonderful man!"

I tried to move, but found I was belted to the bed, that is until later when, as though in a nightmare, Langobard and a pair of Philadelphia constables appeared wearing wreaths of sulfurous air. They hoisted me up. The clamp of a constable's hand on my side called my eyes to what remained of my left arm.

"Oh," I said, looking at the stump in its white bandage, "Oh, my God."

Fifteen

The first cell was the "Tank," a stone chamber with a dozen or so men in the basement of the Philadelphia courthouse. There was a barred window eye-level to the curb. For my first three days, rain poured through. There were no beds. I huddled at the center of the floor. To the extent that I could feel beyond the throb of my stump, I was cold and hungry. To the extent that I could think, I was feverish, confused. English was an alien babble. The men around me traded features, swapping noses, chins. They began the day fat and ended it thin. Their cheeks were creased and their hands gnarled. The bailiffs appeared time and again, top heavy men in caps and bow ties. They bade men out, or brought them in. After a few days, my fever broke, and the nightmare turned dull.

I secured a space against the wall. The wall was a flakey sort of rock that left sparkling dust on your shoulders.

I learned the word *dinner*, our lone meal of the day. The words *mine* and *pot* were important as well. After several more days that don't merit description, a bailiff fetched me to stand before a judge in a sunny courtroom. The judge spoke for a while. Gentlemen on either side of me spoke for a while. The judge spoke for a while again, and the bailiff placed me back in the Tank. The men made room for me along the wall.

"Nowak—psst—Józef Nowak," came a voice from above. Someone in the Tank's window was calling to me. In German, they said, "You, the one-armed Polack!"

"Me?" I asked, looking into the block of daylight.

"Were you on the Meteorite," said the voice, "you, the mutineer?"

"Well, yes, but —"

"C'mere then."

With some caution I went to peer up through the window. Last night, a drunk had pissed through the bars. Often in the day, children pitched rocks down on our heads. Nevertheless, I stood in the light.

In the window was the lower third of a fat man in a brown suit. His shoes were enormous, bulging. His right leg was bracketed in leather and metal, and alongside his left leg was a black cane. This man was Mister Emil Zörner.

"Yes?" I said.

"Emil Zörner. Der Philadelphia Bürger," he said. "I was at your trial. How about getting your story in the newspaper?"

"That was my trial?" I asked. From my vantage,

his brown-suited belly eclipsed the Sun.

"You're in jail and you saw a judge," he said. "What did you think was happening?"

"Some sort of introduction, perhaps?"

"Introduction!" he said with a laugh.

"Did you understand what all was said?" I asked him.

"Of course," he said, "I'm an American."

"Oh," I said.

"You were found guilty," he said.

"Oh," I said.

"Convicted. Attempted murder," he said. "You signed a confession to it, after all."

"Will they hang me?" I said.

"When they get around to it," he said.

I looked to my left arm, or rather to where it used to be, and had the odd sensation that I should apologize to it. The poor thing had been cut away, and now this. I was going to hang.

"But say," said the big man in the window, "how about you tell me your side of the story and I'll put it in the newspaper."

"You're with a newspaper?" I said.

"That's right," he said.

"Which one?"

"Der Philadelphia Bürger," he said with flourish. "A German weekly. Why? Are you some sort of connoisseur of local news outfits?"

"No," I said. "Who are you again?"

"Emil Zörner," he said. "Journalist. Editor. Publisher."

"Oh."

"Listen," he said. "You were squirming all over the courtroom. That stump of yours hurts, no?" He had taken out a jotbook and was thwacking it with a pencil. "Tell me your story, and I'll bring you something for the pain."

I agreed to his terms, adding only that he must bring iodine and bandages, as well. I then told him my story …

On the very next afternoon, Zörner's feet and legs and cane appeared again in the window of the tank. "Mister Nowak," he said. "Delivery for Mister Nowak."

He bent with a groan. The leather and metal of his leg bracket squeaked. "Here," he said. Through the bars he handed me a folded newspaper that clinked. Inside its fold, I discovered four little bottles of laudanum, a bottle of iodine and a roll of clean bandages.

"Hey," he said, catching his breath, still bending, "can you write?"

"Yes," I said.

"Then take this, as well," he said and he held through the bars two sheets of blank paper, bright with the Sun, and a pencil whittled to a point. I took them. The wood of the pencil was a fragrant red cedar. "Write us a letter," he said. "The address of our office is at the top. Make it angry. Don't hold back. Call me fat. Emil Zörner. I'm known for it. Der Bürger loves abuse."

"Thank you," I said.

"Enjoy the dope," he said, and with that he pushed off the wall, squeaked his bracket, and stepped from the curb to ford into a sunlit street and its traffic. He disappeared behind an omnibus.

I opened a bottle of the laudanum and took a sip. It was awful bitter stuff, enough to send you to shudders. I returned to my space at the wall. My neighbors, shoulder to shoulder, eyed me and the remaining bottles as I tucked them behind my back.

First, I set to cleaning my wound. A kind inmate beside me helped pull off my jacket and shirt. The bandage Doctor Davidson had set in place was black and brown with dried and gummed up blood. I unraveled and peeled the bandage from the wound. The pain of the new skin against the air had me gasping, The wound was a thick horseshoe of stitches and dried blood. But there was no stench.

No rot. The wound was healing. Fresh blood beaded up from the blackened cord of scabs. The drainage point, that opening Davidson had left at the intersection of stitches, had a cap of congealed, amber fluid. The skin around the black crust was pale purple. Taut, but not inflamed. I unscrewed the iodine bottle in my teeth and dripped the stuff along the line of the wound. White foam bloomed, hissing, bringing with it a bracing sting. I fumbled with my new bandage until my neighbor again gave me aid. Once the thing was wrapped, he helped me with my shirt and jacket. I gave him a few swigs of laudanum for his trouble. We leaned back against the glittering wall. I read the newspaper that Zörner had given me, Der Philadelphia Bürger, and found myself on the first page below the fold.

One-armed man awaits death. A mutineer, or victim? it asked. I had another sip of laudanum. My eyes roved. Already, the painkiller was at work. *The brute crushed his superior's windpipe like so much brown paper,* Zörner wrote, and somewhere below, he said, *a second man vanished into thin air, or so claims the maimed Polack.*

But this wild account never made it into the court record, Zörner said. *The Polack was overcome by the lingering pain of his amputation, and to the distaste of all present in our good court, the brute moaned and* writhed throughout the trial. The bailiffs were loath to restrain him in his spasms of agony, for even less one arm, the Polack sailor struck a beastly figure, Zörner said.

Later, Zörner asked, *Has not the wretch suffered enough?*

Then, farther down: *Was the captain another villain, in on the plot and closing ranks to dodge American Justice? Or, Dear Reader, is the one-armed man of the Cherry Street jail a savage mutineer?*

I have seen him. One can find this maimed sailor below the grade of the street, prowling by the barred window of his confines. He'll answer to Nowak, his Slavic handle. You may take his mind as spoiled by peasant incest. You may see a farrago artist, or perhaps an honest workman of the sea.

Either way, the Polack is in agony. His eyes burn with a fire. Whether it be the fire of Justice outraged, or the coiled savagery of a degenerate Slav, I leave to you, Dear Reader. In either case, he will hang.

Fighting the nod of the laudanum, I resolved to write Zörner his letter. I saw my fingers around the pencil. I wrote:

Dearest Klara—

Words retreated from me, and in came the nod of the laudanum. I slept, and in my sleep, my fellow inmates took the letter paper and Der Philadelphia

Bürger to wipe their asses as they crouched one by one to shit in the Tank's chamber pot.

A young priest brought me a scapular, believing, I suppose, that it might save me from Hell. His white hand passed the little bundle through the bars of the Tank's window, and he said in Polish, "Pray, my son. Pray to our Lord and you shall be forgiven."

The scapular had a stitching of Saint Sebastian pinned to a tree by arrows. The dye of the wool was fresh and left a crimson circle in my palm.

Sixteen

One morning two bailiffs ushered me from the Tank. I am going to hang, I thought. Outside—at the rear entrance of the courthouse, in a wide stone alley—there stood a horse, a driver, and a black, windowless carriage. A black hood came over my head.

Hands jostled me forward. I was shoved, clipped on the shins, falling into the carriage and its deeper blackness. The door slammed, and off the carriage went, rattling me down the streets of Philadelphia and nearer towards the end. I kicked in a frenzy to gain a footing and throw myself against the door, but succeeded only in hurtling face first against a wall. Stars burst in my head. Blood gushed from my nose and mouth, wetting the hood. I struggled to breathe. The carriage stopped. The door opened. Hands grabbed me by the ankles and yanked me into the open air. I landed on my back and was shouted at and clubbed about the head until I lay still. The black hood was ripped away.

I gulped for air and looked around the white sky. There was no hangman's gibbet

[...]

a massive gatehouse, a castellated tower

[…]

that titanic fortress I had seen at night a month earlier in my first visit to Philadelphia. The Penitentiary

[…]

I would live, interred

[…]

atop its fearsome height was a round chamber of windows, not unlike the lantern room of a lighthouse. At times a guard stood up there behind the glass, or walked out onto a parapet on the wall and stood with his head against the lower portion of the sky

[…]

Pennsylvania has enjoyed renown for its system of enforced penitence, a purgatory often called safe and healthsome, but to my knowledge, no account from a prisoner penitent has made entry into the discussion. Therefore, for posterity, I'll here submit in the remainder of this chapter my own thorough and detailed report

[…]

Seventeen

And so after a time of five months, my imprisonment at the famed Pennsylvania Penitentiary ended.

A door within the dark gatehouse opened, letting in pure white light, and I was pushed out. The door slammed, and there I was, standing on the public curb with my back to the prison walls. Before me was a snow covered avenue, a modest row of houses and shops, windows glaring, roofs padded with snow. The sky was an unbroken chasm of blue.

"Mister Józef Nowak," a man called out.

He crossed the avenue, a stranger to me, and the fact I'd been starved for human society, for faces, for voices, made his strangeness sharper, deeper. Indeed, his image struck my mind as though delivered by a hammer and die.

He was small, with a large head and thin legs, and his hands stuffed deep in his coat pockets.

He stopped some paces before me. His features—nose, mouth and wide set, brown eyes— favored a lower quadrant of his face. And what a forehead! It was occluded by the brim of his derby cap, but gave the impression of prowling thoughts. He spoke German:

"I'm Renner, Edward Renner. Come with me, won't you?"

I stood, blinking like a fool at the sunlight, gasping in the winter air.

"Your luck has turned, Mister Nowak," he said. "Come."

I followed. My feet trod the snow. My ankles were bare. These clothes, a thin brown suit, were not my own. I was soon wet in the shoes.

Looking back, I reckon that Renner had us heading down 21st Street. The neighborhood was then called Charles Hill. These days it's dense with brick, but back then it was a hodgepodge of little wooden homes and bigger manses with bits of acreage. No one was about. Showers of dazzling snow blew from trees and roofs.

Then the character of the neighborhood changed: No trees now, and a bitter fume crept in the cold air. Brick row houses, as though extruded through the city's grid, stood corner to corner. People appeared in doorways.

Renner took me down alleys. American alleys, rectilinear, no medieval mystery. A few more turns and Renner had me in the bustle of a square, a market crowded with hawkers and stalls, the dark shoulders of horses, carriage wheels, women wrapped up and carrying baskets. Seeing me overwhelmed, Renner took me by the sleeve and brought me down a street to a door, which opened and welcomed us into a dark and firewarmed lobby. There were carpets, a stratus of tobacco smoke, a brass or copper chandelier that blazed with a wreath of gas jets. Renner led me up soft stairs. He fished a key from his coat pocket, unlocked and opened a door.

"Is that our man?" said a voice within the room.

I stepped in and found a gentleman in a blue suit. For a moment I was unable to develop an impression of him. The room crawled with patterns: wallpaper of intertwining ivy vines, paisley in the rugs, a checked tablecloth, and white curtains with red flowers. To be sure, it was a normal, well appointed room for a single guest of a moderately-priced inn.

But the blackness and cruelty of the penitentiary had disassembled my senses, unraveled my mind. In truth, I've not fully regained my trust in reality, in gravity, in the order of the Earth and sky, or in time, that one thing follows another. So I was then: confused. Also, I was standing in wet boots and too small a suit.

"Ah, yes, that's him," said the gentleman. "Well done, Renner."

"Thank you, Mister Persson."

Person? Persson.

Even prompted by the name, my eyes did not register the man. Not immediately. On the Meteorite, I had steered clear of Persson and had, as I've said, a bad feeling about him. The bile we taste for life's little despots. Yet I had taken note of his face, that smooth and unnerving perfection. Now this face was before me, set with those tilted, blue or green eyes.

He invited me to sit, and so we sat, and he drummed his fingers on the hollow of his hat. He was suited up, spats to collar and cuffs, and had slicked his hair.

"Józef Nowak," he said. "Józef. I'll call you Józio," he said.

I've never cared for that derivation.

"Józio," he said, "let's skip the mystery." He smiled and raised a hand, as though he were about to make the sign of the cross. "I was the one that set you free."

He did resemble, in his small perfection, the infant Jesus.

"Well?" he said.

"Am I free?"

"Yes," he said.

It brings me no pleasure to report how I abased myself.

"Thank you, sir!" I cried. "Thank you, Mister Persson!"

I fell out of the chair and onto my knees. A full kowtow upon the carpet. Oh, the warm tears, as though issuing from cracks at my core.

Persson was chuckling. "Oh, bless you, poor Józio, bless you! Look at what a bit of time on ice does to a man!"

He and Renner helped me back into the chair. I raised my eyes and asked, in trembles, "How did you get me out, Mister Persson?"

"Money and connections, Józio," he said, wagging his head and smiling. "My father's influence," he said, "prudently strained."

There was more to it than that.

"So," I said, "they won't hang me?"

Lord! How I shook!

Persson laughed. "No, Józio, they won't hang you. You've been—what's the word—*exonerated*, and what's more," he said, "I'm going to get you a job."

"Thank you, sir!"

He gestured my thanks away. "Please. It's obvious that an injustice was done. I mean, look at you," he said, motioning towards the ghost of my left arm. "It was combat between men, no?"

"Yessir," I said.

"And didn't Dudko have you at the fire without break or water?"

"Yessir."

"For nights in a row?"

I nodded.

"You see," he said, "that was the first blow! And Dudko struck it. Might have killed a lesser man, Józio."

A talented actor that Persson! How, without a qualm, he concealed his role! But I outpace myself.

I recall that at Persson's next gesture, I flinched.

He reached over and patted me on the shoulder. His hand was like an iron mitt. "But you survived the furnace, then the knife, and now the prison," he said. Those eyes of his sparkled. "One can't help but conclude that you're ordained for greater things, Józio."

"Thank you, sir," I managed. Pitiful.

"So," he said, standing from the chair and donning his overcoat, "I can't stay. I'm going to see about this job for you, whether we can line it all up. It's not on a ship, of course." He inspected his derby and lowered it onto his dark blonde crown. "Your adventure has come ashore, Józio. Understand?"

"Yessir."

He strode towards the door, but halted.

"This job, Józio, if I decide you're right for it, well, it's confidential in nature, sensitive, and will require you to be, to be pliant."

"Yessir," I said.

"Oh, and Józio," he said, looking at me, "do you recall the woman who tended your wound in the sickbay aboard the Meteorite?"

"The nurse, sir?"

"No, not that old woman," he said. "There was a tall woman with dark hair. She seemed to know you."

Could it be?

"Rather impressive stature, this woman," he said.

Could Klara have followed me? Could she have followed me onto Meteorite?

Outwardly, I betrayed nothing. "Sorry, sir, I don't recall her," I said. "Though I was in quite a fever."

Persson smiled and nodded. "Very well then, Józio, but listen," he said, now standing in the hallway. "Don't go anywhere. Stay right here. Supper will be up in a few hours. Renner and I will check on you. Adieu for now, Józef Nowak," he said, and before leaving with Renner, he raised a gloved hand in a sort of salute, or, again, a blessing.

Eighteen

That afternoon, rain fell and washed away the snow. A mist filled the windows and later froze in a pattern resembling flowers in a meadow.

This room was on the second floor of the Strangers Union, an inn on 17th Street. I've passed by it many times in the years since. I recall the supper that evening, a wonderful leek and potato soup with black bread and sugared butter. It went down without a hitch. The proprietor himself came to clear away the dishes, whereupon he remarked on the chill of the room, and soon returned with fuel for the little black stove in the corner. He was a thin and stooped man, a Bavarian that spoke in a rounded melody, and he often clapped as he set about making the fire, arranging split logs and kindling and paper, all while welcoming me to Philadelphia and telling me how a man might get ahead. He recommended the felt trade for hats. The flames were going now, roaring within that black iron box. The fire filled his spectacles. "You say you're of Polish breed?" he said.

"Yes. From Bialystok," I said. "Do you know it?"

"And you say," he continued, "that you're a sailor?"

"Until recently," I said.

The proprietor looked down for an instant. He had a wadded bit of newspaper in his hands.

"It's a fine place you have, sir," I said. "Probably don't get many sailors."

Without a word more, he stood up. The kindling lay pell mell on the rug, but he left at once, hugging one last unused old newspaper to his chest.

I recall the room had a painting of a shack in a field of wheat, or in a desert. The painting hung on the wall between the windows. It seemed a third and smaller window, one that looked far across the continent. From the shack, a figure was staring out, but the figure was at odds with the scale of the shack, as though he were an adult caught within a child's playhouse.

I was sane, more or less, yet I passed hours gazing into that painting.

A little after night fell on the following day, Renner came to the room with a large brown package in his hands. "From Mister Persson," he said.

It was a full suit of clothes: stockings, a shirt and sleeves, a black vest, a jacket and pants, and a greatcoat with its left sleeve already pinned up. "And these," Renner said, handing me a pair of boots. "Put it all on," he said, "I'm to see that it fits."

I stripped down and began the tedious challenge of getting dressed with one arm. Meanwhile, Renner sat in the chair by the stove. It had a high back, forming a sort of dark cocoon in which his hands and head, that grand dome and downward settled face, floated.

"Can you write, Mister Nowak?"

"I was educated in letters," I replied, as I guided my foot into a pant leg.

"How's that?" he asked.

"Monks. I was raised by the monastic order of Basilians. Outside of Bialystok."

"Can you take orders?" he said.

"Absolutely," I said. "I was a soldier."

"A soldier for whom?"

"The Free Poland Militia."

"And what did you do?"

"Reconnaissance," I said. "A scout."

"Perfect," said Renner, shifting in the chair, moving his pale face forward from the dark cocoon. He then asked whether I was married, or had ever been married, whether I had children, any bastards, any parents alive, any brother or sisters. I sat down. No, I said, again and again as the questions came to me.

"So, you have no one at all," Renner said.

"That's right," I said.

"Lastly," said Renner, "and here's the job, there's a woman Persson wants you to find…"

The whole of me was taken in a cold shudder.

"Her name," he said, "is Klara Glockner."

The name exploded in my heart.

He described her physically, though not to the standard of a devotee.

"Resident of Danzig," he concluded, "a Kashubian, passenger of the Meteorite five months ago. That's the job. Find this woman. You want it?"

"Yes," I said..

Renner, still just hands and a head in the dark of the chair, chuckled.

"For some reason, Nowak," he said, "Mister Persson believes in you. He believes you have a spiritual connection to this woman. This connection, Mister Persson says, will guide you. He's quite mystical."

"Mister Renner," I said. "What's your line of work? You're a detective, aren't you?"

Renner smiled.

"How would you go find this woman?" I asked.

Renner stood from the cocoon of the chair. He put his derby on, pulling the band of it to hide that enormous forehead. "Start at the docks," he said, "look amongst the whores."

Renner was a rather poor detective. That night, he did not realize that I followed him out of the Strangers Union, down Chestnut Street and to a hotel, The Continental House, and its restaurant where Persson was dining alone by candlelight. Renner reported to Persson and left him to finish the meal. I waited in the shadow of an alley. The greatcoat was wonderfully warm, and the boots, though stiff, kept the water out. A while later, Persson left the restaurant and walked to his hotel. He made two stops:

First, he paused to consider some wretches around a bonfire.

Second, he stopped before a church.

The church had a broad bank of steps to three red doors that wore fir wreaths. To the side, on a little plot of grass, someone had erected a nativity scene. I hadn't realized that Christmas was so near. Joseph and Mary and the assorted animals were painted onto planks of wood and speared into ground. Most were already leaning backwards or forwards, the ground having softened with rain. The manger was absent of Jesus.

Nineteen

[...]

Over the bridge, herdsmen drove sheep into the city.

[...]

Schuylkill River, black and low in its banks.

[...]

Church steeples and the blockish horde

[...]

But then the Medical College of the University of Pennsylvania, a fearsome green building amid snowy lawns

[...]

Inside, tidily coiffed young men loitered

[...]

the lecture hall's steep stands of pews. The Anatomies of Abnormality

[...]

hand to hand, jars were making their way

[...]

suspended in green liquid was a fetus, a pale thing without features, save two slits for eyes.

[...]

I could never be a physician. The profession implies too frank a truth.

[...]

lay a blanket over the jars

[...]

as though to put the odd, preserved infants to sleep.

[...]

the professor. Sunlight brightened his white hair as it would a cloud. It shone in his spectacles

[…]

"Excuse me," I said, "Doctor Davidson?"

[…]

Meyn Got!"

[…]

it took the time of several beers to explain. He swept clean arcs in the broken peanut shells between us. His voice bounded between shouts and whispers. A few of the tavern's quieter patrons were eyeballing us.

"Doctor," I said, "there was a woman —"

"Klara!" he said, spilling a bit of beer.

"Yes!" I said, throwing a napkin on the spill, "That's her name, Klara —"

"What a mysterious woman! I spoke with her at length as she tended to you, but that nurse—the old woman, do you recall?—she despised you! The nurse, I mean." His gaze dropped off the table.

"She took care of me? Klara, I mean."

"Oh yes," he said, "in your fever."

"Doctor, I have to find her. Do you know where she is?"

"No."

"Oh," I responded, and I did not press. I am not a natural investigator.

We fell silent for a while and worked at our beers. Davidson gazed off for a moment, looking somewhere within the flames of a chandelier over the bar. He signaled the barman for another round. The beers arrived.

"Józef," said the doctor, "how is it that—?"

"That I'm free?"

"Yes!"

"A rich man named Persson got me out. He was on the Meteorite. His father owned it."

"A person freed you?" Davidson said. "But how?"

"With money."

"Money? That's not how the justice system works!" the doctor protested. Then he looked at the peanut shells, as though reading them. "This person must know something," he said, "Perhaps he—perhaps he was involved."

"Involved?" I said. "What do you mean?"

"I don't know, but Józef," Davidson said, "perhaps you'd do better to return to Danzig?"

Davidson went on about Danzig, that watery city, and he spoke of the Long Market and the quay, and the nest of streets between, and of his brothers, their business concerns. He said that they'd have use of a keen, young man, and that he could write a letter of introduction. I was still so young, he said, and could have a new start of things.

I half-listened.

Davidson tilted his beer glass. It was empty and he frowned at the bottom. He raised his hand for another drink. Peanut shells were now stuck to his sleeve. He dropped his hand, abandoning the idea of more beer. He looked at me and shook his head. "Cursed age, Józef," he said. "Cursed age. Time, time, time."

A few moments later and we were out in the cold. Davidson waved down a hack. During our time in the tavern, the Sun had vanished, and slush had frozen to grey and black, covering the city streets. The hack slid sideways to the curb as it stopped. Church bells tolled six o'clock. Davidson climbed aboard and held open the door to the carriage. "Come on then."

I climbed in after him. Seated in the darkness, moving somewhere through Philadelphia, Davidson reached over and touched my shoulder. "May I?" he asked.

"Yes," I said, knowing that he wanted to see the stump. I felt unusually close to the man. Moreover, I was a bit drunk. As the carriage rattled down streets, I partly undressed and bared my wound.

Davidson crouched in the space between our carriage benches. He held my knee. He struck me for a moment as a character from a child's tale, an old elf, or an intelligent vole. In the swipes of passing streetlamps, he examined the trunk of muscle and bone and the scars of his handiwork. He fumbled in his pockets and retrieved a tin. From it he put two tiny white cubes in the palm of my hand.

"For the pain," he said. "You chew them."

I tossed them back, and their power crept out from my teeth.

"Morphine," said Davidson. He tipped a few into his own palm and climbed back onto his bench. "Quite safe," he said, chewing.

[...]

before his home, a towering thing that reared back from the street like a spooked horse.

[...]

an old Irish woman named Anne, Davidson's maid. She had a musical laugh. She served us pie. Later, still in full dress, I fell onto a bed somewhere in the remote heights of the house.

I awoke, and beyond the window, the Moon as though made of lye, burned. The sky's dark vault turned. The Moon left the window's high pane. I stalked out of the room and through the house. I pushed open doors with my fingertips, and on the second floor, in a master bedroom overlooking the blackened street, Doctor Davidson sat propped up in his bed, reading by the light of a lamp. A tidy pile of glowing logs crackled in the fireplace. Davidson wore a stocking cap and a blanket around his shoulders. Catching sight of me, he asked, "Trouble sleeping, Józef?"

The fire reflected in his spectacles.

[...]

"Józef," he said, "have you ever lost time?"

"How do you mean, doctor?"

"I mean," he said, leaning forth, "to have gone from one moment to the next and found that hours, or even days, have disappeared.

[...]

Not in the banal sense wherein your mind wanders," he said. "Rather, I speak of a break where your conscious experience ceases, then resumes much later, often in a different place and with no interlude."

"Yes, doctor," I said. "I have."

"You're not alone," he said. "There's thousands

upon thousands of you!"

"What do you mean, doctor?" I said.

"In my studies, I've discovered that some of you, the people that suffer lost time, also experience a sub-condition, a contingent and extraordinary condition. I call it *advenus raptio*."

The fire cracked.

"*Advenus raptio*," I said. "You mean I've been … kidnapped?"

"Ah!" he said. "You have your Latin! Yes," he said. "Kidnapped. Other investigators and theorists have called it *exastia* or *anime a corpore abstractus*." He tapped the book on his lap. "But I believe it's bodily. No mere trick of the mind, rather a literal *trance* as in a transition to another place. You're taken somewhere."

I began to sweat. The fire was cooking my kneecaps. I did not understand what he was on about.

"*Amisit tempore*," I said.

"Time lost," the doctor said. "At the very least."

A log slumped in the hearth, sending out a hush and flight of sparks, one of which died on the rug. The doctor and I watched.

"Give the fire a poke, will you Józef?" said Davidson.

I got up, took the poker and stirred sparks from

around the dead edges of the fire. The logs shifted and freed a flame at the center of the hearth. It flowered up from the glowing, dark wood.

"And you believe," I said, "that Klara and I share this condition —"

"*Advenus raptio*," the doctor said.

"— that we are kidnapped and returned."

"I suspect it," he said.

"But by whom?"

"I wouldn't yet hazard a guess," he said. He tilted the book on his lap to my eyes. It was not a printed volume, but a thick sheaf of notes, pages packed with handscript. "But I shall find out," he said. "It's my life's work."

"Doctor," I said, "is this why I can't find her?"

"Oh, Józef, you've just begun looking."

Twenty

[...]

T he following day
[...]

an untrammeled blue morning
[...]

clouds stretching in the distance
[...]

windows over the street as flashing blades.
[...]

into a slum. I passed a ruined church, blackened by fire. Dogs circled in the street. They snarled at me. Other people were out. They stood still. From behind walls came screams and shouts. The Sun went down.
[...]

Philadelphia, you are cursed
[...]

Back then, nuns went patrolling, looking for poor women who were alone and out of doors
[...]

Doors unlocked in the surrounding buildings. People trickled out, people who hustled, eyes down and away from the dawn. I moved with them like a branch fallen into a river.
[...]

came days without consequence. I checked every saloon, reasoning that she might have taken up her old trade. I asked at women's boarding houses. I even took Renner's advice and looked amongst the professional women at the

[...]

Twenty-one

Yet later that night, when neither a soul nor a tumbling leaf stirred on the streets, I knocked on a door. Its glazing read in silver-painted letters: Der Philadelphia Bürger. From behind those letters came the glow of a burning lamp, and Emil Zörner, journalist, editor, publisher, opened the door.

"You," he said.

Zörner was a huge man. Just below my height, but worth four of me in girth, he stood in his shirt sleeves with a green eyeshade tilted across his brow. Zörner's eyes were small, fragile things. Then, with an ink-stained finger, he reached out and prodded my shoulder. "Well," he said, "you don't seem a ghost."

"I remembered the address," I said.

"So," he said, "it's me you'll haunt. Come in."

That night Zörner served me tea with sugar. We sat by the stove and inaugurated what would later become a routine feature of our lives: sprawling talks through the dark hours.

Allow me to share a kaleidoscope's view of my friend Emil Zörner, some of which I gleaned that night:

Emil was born in a village near Munich in 1832. His father had been away for two years as a Hussar cavalryman for the Army. When he returned, he took the infant Emil from his wife's arms. Emil's right leg was deformed, twisted. His mother swore that she had been true, that the conception was immaculate. The Hussar rode off with the infant Emil towards some tributary of the Danube, intending to throw him in, but on the way he softened to the bastard. He resigned from the Calvary and became a schoolteacher, then a judge. Emil grew up, went to Munich and joined a seminary. The Revolution of May 1848 followed close behind. Emil hid first in a laundry, then fled the city and hid in a hay barn. The Revolution passed. Emil failed out of the seminary and found work as a printer. His mother and sister came to live with him, bearing the news that his father had died. Emil's sister was in bloom, and was soon engaged to a man well positioned in the railroad business, which had only then penetrated the hills between Munich and Nuremberg. Shortly after the wedding, Emil's mother fell before a tram, another novelty, and it crushed her. Her ghost visited Emil and told him that she had read the manuscript he was writing about his father's life. It's trash, his mother's ghost said. Emil soonafter dropped the manuscript in the Isar River and went to America. In Philadelphia, he worked as a printer and then a reporter for Die Republik, the city's foremost German newspaper. The spirit of his father, which paced within Emil's soul, snarled at Die Republik's editors, for down to a man they were political and literary cowards. After a dozen years of bowing and scraping before them, Emil set out on his own and founded Der Philadelphia Bürger. By the time I appeared in Der Bürger's pages as the mutinous Polack, the paper had run for over ten years. It tasked a small staff and came out weekly. It favored stories longer than those in Die Republik. More grotesque and speculative, Zörner would admit. Jailhouse tales were a favourite, a stock-in-trade, so my tale of woe was one of many. I was the first of these subjects, however, to come calling at Der Bürger's door on 22nd Street.

I told him of Klara, that I was searching for her. I told Zörner everything. He was a talented confessor.

By then the night had passed and a pale and dirty dawn had begun beyond the windows of the office. Carriage, cart and foot traffic had started in the street. Inside, Der Burger's small office—desks, lamps and papers—took shape in the morning light. Zörner was frowning at my tale

[...]

"Don't despair," said Zörner, patting me on the

knee. "Write down what you know, and I'll make inquiries."

After one last cup of tea, Zörner arranged me at a desk with paper and pen. At his urging, I attempted to put in plain order what had happened and what I had learned. My mind kept slipping between the Meteorite, Danzig, the eastern forests and the monastery, my lost arm. Meanwhile, in filtered Der Bürger's staff, a few clerks and reporters. They scratched away. They scurried around the office, its jumble of desks.

Hours later in my task, I stopped and read what I had written. My life as a mad scrawl. It was worse than I could have imagined.

[...]

Zörner, holding the pages in his paws, squinted down his nose and read. "Nice penmanship," he said. "How would you like a job?"

TWENTY-TWO

One night in Davidson's house, I stood by the window overlooking the yard and the dark backs of neighboring homes, three-story affairs joined by party walls, gabled and peaked, and capped by a thin blanket of snow charged blue by the Moon. My ghost arm vibrated at the end of my stump.

A noise, a groan in a floor board, occurred behind me.

Someone had come up the rear stairs within Davidson's house. They moved first upon the treads of the staircase and now upon the floorboards of the landing, adding so slightly to the timber's burden. The movement had been too fast and light to have been the doctor, or his maid Anne. This roving entity—I was open at that moment to the metaphysical— approached and then stopped at the door.

I sensed that this entity sensed me standing there.

One has a larger sphere of sensation when awake in a house at night.

The entity left.

It descended the stairs of the house and crossed the ground floor, passing into realms my senses could not follow.

But then a door closed at the rear of the house and a creature flitted into the moonpatch of the yard.

The thing was a man, hatless and baldheaded.

For a moment, I thought I must be dreaming.

But the moment passed, and I went after him. I descended the stairs and ran out into the yard. He was gone, but then someone moved in the dark of the alley, and the man appeared for a moment beneath a streetlamp.

I was off like a shot, but the bare-headed man was fleet-footed. Up a steep street, he expanded the distance between us to a full block. I felt as though I were running backward. But I kept sight of him, bright as the night was with the aid of the Moon and snow.

He ran by the stone gate of a cemetery, down a street of unlit houses, and was soon sprinting into the white lawn of the University. My mind emptied as I put on speed. But I could see that the man was leading, not escaping. To wit, he stopped for a moment to mark my pursuit.

He took off again, and I found myself rounding a corner, whereupon a crowd appeared and lights blazed from the open doors of a church. An organ blasted from within, and every person issuing from the light was singing, wishing each other glad tidings, donning shawls and coats and scarves and linking arms. It was Christmas Eve!

I vaulted up the steps and looked around for my man.

He was beyond the crowd, out in the moonlight.

The chase resumed, and soon we were crossing a stone bridge. The black Schuylkill ran beneath us.

At the end of the bridge, he took a stairway down into the dark maze of lanes and hovels that spread along the riverside. My lungs burned. I had sweated into my clothes and that sweat had chilled. The man, partways up a block, entered a building.

I came upon the door. An evergreen wreath hung upon it, and music played within. From the black and cold street, I went in and reeled from the heat, golden light, song and life. It was a dining hall, festooned for the holiday with candles and holly and ribbon, and packed with revelers.

The man who had led me there was nowhere to be seen. I recall that in an instant, the master of the house, a round-faced man with a mustache, took me by the elbow, ushering me in towards a place at a long table, where another man was looking up, beaming, with cabbage across his beard.

I said, "Please, no food, sir."

A thought formed: *Klara was here.*

The man in the night had led me to Klara.

With this thought, the dining hall became a mad wall of color, light and noise. There were sparkling eyes and mouths around me, the aroma of meat and vinegar, a mirror behind the bar ablaze with light, the master of the house's hand on my back, but where among it all was Klara?

I turned a swift step and found before me a very different woman.

She was small, pale and old and wore a white bonnet and a black dress. "Oh my," she said, "I never thought I'd see you again!"

Her hand shot out and grabbed my wrist.

I did not recognize her.

"You speak German?" I said.

"Of course," the woman said, "and French, and English, and Greek, and —"

"Forgive me," I said, still looking about, "but have you seen a man?"

"Yes," she replied, "I've seen a man."

"A specific man, I mean. Bareheaded," I said. "And baldheaded."

The woman pointed to the aforementioned man with cabbage in his beard. He was baldheaded.

"The man I'm looking for just ran in," I said.

"Sailor Nowak!" she cried with a laugh. It gave

me a jolt, this woman knowing me. Her mouth flickered as she spoke. "Are you not at all surprised to see me?"

"Pardon?" I said.

"I know you intimately," she said. The bones of her hand cinched my wrist. Her hand was cold.

"From the Meteorite," she said.

This woman was Nurse Kindersley.

"Nurse… Kindersley?" I ventured, searching my mind.

"I must say," she said, "I am thunderstruck. How is it you are in the great wide world? How is it, Nowak, that you are alive? I'd heard," she said, tugging my wrist, "that you were, at the very least, in the *stone jug*."

"In the what?"

"Isn't that what they call it? Prison?" She was smiling, quite like a possum, or a snake. "Oh, do sit with me, Nowak. Sit with an old woman," she said. "You're such a young and handsome man, and so tall."

A thought came to me: Klara tended to me in the Meterorite's sickbay. The sickbay was Nurse Kingersley's realm. Ergo, she must know Klara.

"You know," the nurse said to me, having led me to a chair and taken a place across from me, "I think it suits you, being less one arm."

"Madam, Nurse Kindersley, have you seen a woman named Klara Glockner? She was on the Meteorite. She's tall with dark hair and she —"

Nurse Kindersley smiled. "Yes, Józef. I have seen her."

"Where is she?"

"She is gone, Józef."

"Where?"

"She went back to Prussia, back to Danzig, for you were in jail, you poor man," Kindersley said, "and surely you wouldn't ask that she —"

The nurse was lying. I was certain of it. Klara might even be near, perhaps in that very room in the crowd of diners and revelers, the raised glasses, carolers, mistletoe and candles. The nurse grabbed my sleeve.

"How did you get out? Tell me. You were convicted. You were going to hang."

"Mister Persson," I said.

"Mikkal Persson?"

"Yes," I said, still looking about the room. "He arranged for my, what's the word, *exoneration*

[...]

Persson.

[...]

I went out into the night.

[...]

The lounge was dark as a cave

[...]

Spats to collar, Persson was dollhouse perfection.

[...]

horse tackle hung from the paneled walls, bugles, stirrups and whatnot.

Renner was about the dark room looking for matches or a tinderbox.

[...]

"So, Józio," said Persson, "you say she's lying. The nurse, you say, is concealing Klara from us."

"Rather concealing Klara from me," I said. "To you, I believe, the nurse would reveal her

[...]

Persson lit his pipe, cupping the bowl, and blew a spark from his thumb.

[...]

"Nurse Kindersley delivered me," he said. "She brought me into this world."

[...]

I looked to the fire, a handsome blaze of black quarter logs. On the nearer side of the fireplace hung the familiar tools: a brush, a shovel and the stoker.

[...]

Beware the Jew doctor, Józio," Persson said, "Jakub Davidson is a Luciferian. A Satanist."

He shifted in his cushioned throne, then grimaced and shifted again. At the time I imagined he had a cramp, or an injured hip. Looking back I realize that an object dug into his ribs. Persson was wearing a gun.

[...]

you must discover Davidson's designs. For Klara's sake, Józio."

[...]

The lounge had emptied out. In the last several minutes, the door had opened again and again, letting in shocks of daylight.

By the far wall, at a bar, a tender was polishing glasses. Near him, a gentleman slouched against the brass rail. All around the walls were paintings, landscapes, likely with hunting scenes in the foreground. In one, the closest, the red tongue of a hound shown within its black mouth.

Renner stood near me. He counted out a fold of banknotes.

"You've done good work, Józio," Persson said.

Renner held the counted notes out to me. Within them, I'd soon discover, the detective had enclosed a message.

Twenty-three

[...]

We walked away from the crowd
[...]

dogs skulking, loping with noses low at a market on the western edge of the city
[...]

prams over frozen ruts of mud and a derelict who wore a blanket for trousers.
[...]

Tall birch trees, bare against the white sky, scrolls of bark upon the frozen grass
[...]

You told me you were raised by monks," Renner said. "Were you an orphan?"
[...]

Persson and Kindersley were in league
[...]

"They have Klara?"

"Yes."
[...]

the list consisted of trains and their destinations, an itinerary that crossed Pennsylvania to the start of the Middle West, went south to the Gulf of Mexico, and then west across Texas and into the

desert territories. "That's where they're going,"
Renner said.

[...]

If I should tell you, and you don't catch them

[...]

To my surprise, the man was crying.

[...]

"Cholera," he said.

[...]

wife, daughter

[...]

dead."

[Third Folio—Intact]

Twenty-four

The next day found Doctor Davidson and I beneath soot-darkened flags on Platform 4 at Philadelphia's Centennial Rail Station. Our train was the Silver Glade, though it was green, and it lay empty and locked in wait of its conductors, valets and attendants. This was the first train in our pursuit of Kindersley, Persson and Klara, and it would be the first train I had ever boarded. I knew the smell of burning coal, the acrid dust and the fume of engine metal, but the rest was strange, principally the metallic screeches near and far and the odd stillness in the repose of train carriages.

I recall that the sky at the high and open back of the rail hall was turning to an early, overcast evening. Falling snow was turning to rain.

Over a few minutes, the platform swelled with passengers. Red-capped attendants came hurrying through the crowd, and people shouted after them. The crowd had come from a connecting train from New York or Baltimore, and it had arrived either late or early, and now the Silver Glade would carry double capacity.

I worried that we would lose our place on the train, but Doctor Davidson assured me that we would get aboard, and moreover he explained that such circumstances were an ally to us, for if we followed the route Renner had provided, a delay or missed connection ahead of us would give us the opportunity to catch up with Klara, say in Nashville, or Mobile, or Dallas. In all likelihood, he said, we'd find her on a crowded platform, waiting on a late train.

Whistles sounded, and the attendants climbed the steps of the train, and after them came a great push. Parents shouted and held aloft their small children. The attendants disappeared into the trains. Cries of protest rose up. Doctor Davidson, who was seasoned in all manner of travel, said to me that if I could stay with the luggage for a few minutes, he could get a seat somewhere ahead. I said, "Of course, doctor," and as though by a secret passageway, Davidson was gone. The luggage wasn't much. A single carpet bag and a trunk. The train doors then opened and the attendants called out, "All aboard!"

I called out to the doctor. He did not appear.

One man came forward with his family in tow. His wife was clutching three children. He was shouting at his brood to hurry. He was a gentleman, but the sort that forgoes decorum because he believes that others have none. Before me was an elderly couple, looking at turns to their tickets and to the glut of people and bags now boarding the Silver Glade. I could not move around them. I waited. From the engine came a hiss and clang, hiss and clang, hiss-clang, hiss-clang. White steam flooded up from beneath the platform and its wet heat wove through our legs. Black steam flowed above us, blocking the lamps. It came with the peppery taste of coal. The crowd coughed, sneezed and spat.

I called again for the doctor. Again, he did not appear.

Attendants came through the dirty mist, checking tickets. The platform thinned as the windows of the train filled with faces. I thought to call the doctor again, but reasoned that I would find him on the train. A valet, a Negro with a satin vest and a great belly, stepped up and hoisted the trunk from beneath me, somehow without chucking me on the chin or knocking off my hat, and he steered me through the steam to an attendant at a door three cars away. I dropped the bag and slapped my pockets for my ticket book.

The attendant, a Negro, as well, this one with yellowy eyes and a fine mustache, simply stared at me a while. His face was wet from the steam, or from sweat. "We're boarding now, sir," he said. "Ticket please."

A bell from the engine rang.

I searched myself again, but found no ticket.

The valet dropped the trunk behind me. The attendant turned to other passengers who had their tickets at the ready. They boarded. My heart thrashed in my chest. Had the doctor gone off with my ticket book?

A whistle let out a mournful howl. A great flood of pure white steam swallowed me to the waist. The Negro attendant turned back to face me and, as though he were a magician, he pulled my ticket from the chest pocket of my coat. "Come aboard, sir," he said.

I climbed the nearest steps into the train and pressed into the standing crowd at the back of a car. My neighbors glared at me. I had the handle of the carpet bag in my teeth and the trunk beneath my arm. The doors slammed. The Silver Glade's iron wheels turned, the train shook—it was much like a ship—and our motion west began.

Having never traveled by train, the etiquette was unknown to me. Could one move about? I stood, sweating, clutching the luggage. My neighbors did the same. I began to worry: What if Doctor Davidson thought that I never made it aboard? Would he get off at the first stop and take the next train back? My worry became a panic, soon intolerable, but then a man pushed through the crowd. He pulled on the door, a thick metal affair, and let it slam behind him. Several of us followed his lead. One by one we stepped out of that car, through the door and onto the short gangway between cars, exposed to the air.

I breathed in the cold sky and the cinder smoke. Metal plates shifted beneath my feet. The train screamed around a curve. We had speed now. Philadelphia, already distant, was a dim glow over a dark slant of earth.

I passed into the next car. Witness Józef Nowak, an oversized one-armed man hauling luggage down the lengths of a jolting, swaying, body-crowded train car. Angry oaths followed me. With the bag's handle between my teeth like a bit, I begged forgiveness. At last, after shouldering my way through several cars, I saw Doctor Davidson.

He waved and smiled.

With some help, I got the trunk and bag into the rack above and found a seat. The man beside me shouted, "I'm headed for Wyoming!" He had a gnarled face, a chaotic beard and a suit that smelled powerfully of onions.

"Wyoming? My, how nice," I replied. My English was improving.

"*Nice?*" he shouted. "Who in the Hell said

Wyoming was *nice*?"

It was suddenly obvious why the seat had been vacant.

The man hopped up and pulled a gunny bag down from the rack. In so doing, he elbowed me on the head. He opened the sack, releasing a deeper stench of onion, and squirreled through his belongings. A conductor passed in the aisle, and my neighbor spun on his heel. "Sir," he yelled to the conductor, "sir, can we not burn something more fragrant in yon stove?"—There was a little black heat stove by the door.—"Whyn't cedar?" he shouted "Or applewood, say?"

The conductor passed out of the car without reply. My neighbor swore an oath after him and then shoved the gunny bag back up onto the rack. Once again, he knocked me on the head. I stared at him. He stared back and exuded his oniony stink.

Night came. We were passing through Pennsylvania's modest mountains. They bristled with empty trees. Towns appeared in the moonlit hollows.

I took from my coat pocket a length of pencil and the jotbook Zörner had given me. I wanted to capture something of the moment.

"Józef. Józef." The doctor was standing in the

aisle. "Where's the bag?"

I stood and fetched the bag from the rack.

The doctor dug through the bag's contents and fished out his tin of tablets. He shuttled three or four of its tiny cubes into his mouth and rested a moment, chewing the morphine. He passed me a few. With their help, I slept.

While I was asleep, we stopped in Pittsburgh. My neighbor squirmed against me. I awoke to the Sun in full bearing. Sweat soaked through my clothes. My neighbor shouted, "Where the boy wit dem oranges?" and then commenced to whistle an aimless melody between his teeth. I put my head to the window and watched the towns pass. Some of their names borrowed glory. See Vienna, Athens. Others came from another world of sound. Shawnee, Chillicothe. I recall a town called Loveland.

At some point, whilst the train made its way through hill after hill, I was suddenly convinced that we had missed Cincinnati where we were due to switch trains.

I got up, pushed past my neighbor and stepped into the aisle.

"Damn you, you foreigner!" he shouted.

I pulled the luggage from the rack and at the same moment, a Negro man with a green cap and vest, an attendant or conductor, appeared in the aisle. He shielded his head at my tottering approach.

"Cincinnati?" I said.

"Next stop," he said.

In Cincinnati, on the platform, I looked for Klara, but did not find her.

The doctor and I had a long wait, and he treated me to supper in the station cafe. I was both bone-tired and wild, that odd mixture one gets with travel, and so excused myself to stroll the station in an effort to right the scales. The station, for the most part, was a cold expanse left to the society of pigeons and sparrows.

The board then announced our southbound vessel: The Hummingbird.

From that night aboard the train I recall the Ohio River, the watery plain of it, its path of moonlight through the hills. Somewhere on the edge of Kentucky, the lights of a small city wrapped around the river. The train slowed and pulled from the river with a metallic whine, and we came into a train yard and moved slowly, as though lost.

Low buildings came on either side and narrowed on us. We hissed to a halt at a station, no more than a pass-through platform at the edge of the town.

Little boys boarded our train and came down the aisle selling old newspapers. The whistle sounded and the boys left. We pulled out of the station.

The train crept through the remainder of the town and we re-entered the countryside, though we stayed slow. There was some whispered talk throughout the car, but it died. On occasion, a house appeared in a broad, moonlit yard.

The train was hurtling again, now down a corridor of straight black trees. The ground beneath bucked, and we all rose an inch from our seats. The small door of the heat stove yawned open. Nothing, no flames or embers. A baby began to fuss.

Later, the train stopped. The doctor and I got off to stretch our legs. It was a lone platform in the wilderness. From the night came the yips and howls of coyotes, wolves, or dogs. At the end of the platform, the rail lines cleaved the black forest in two. The lines went off into nothing.

For a while, I had no thoughts of who I was or what I was doing.

We boarded the train, and the journey south resumed. The trees fell away. The train was coming around on a hillside. The Moon was high, a nick of platinum. It moved over a valley in halos, brightening the tops of trees.

As a boy I ran in the hills and woods north of

Bialystok. That night on the Hummingbird, these American forests seemed quite the same. I fell asleep.

A day and a night later, we disembarked at the Hummingbird's terminus, New Orleans, Louisiana. The station was like a Roman temple, but after the fall. The doctor reasoned that if we stayed in the station and took the first departure on the south Texas line, we'd gain half a day in our pursuit. I agreed, of course, and stood guard while he slept fitfully on a bench.

At dawn, a flock of Negro boys whisked through the station with brooms and pans. The stands and ticket counters opened. People appeared, trains awoke, and the place assumed the look of a proper station.

We boarded our train west. It went by the name Texas Eagle, and it flew through a landscape of swamp rivers, dead vines and bare, brittle trees. My exhaustion doubled, and it struck me that our project—to race across this emptiness in search of Klara—was insanity.

A strange man sat across from the doctor and me.

"My name is James Derrick," he said, "from Dakota," and he added, "I'm a Sioux."

"I'm a Jew," rejoined Davidson.

"But where are you from?" asked Derrick.

"Philadelphia," said Davidson.

"Oh, how terrible," said Derrick. He then looked to me.

I told him I was from Poland. "It's a country that does not exist," I said.

Derrick wore a suit, a little too large. A scar divided his forehead, running from his hatband to the bridge of his nose.

"Are you a Jew, as well?" he asked.

"Maybe," I said. "I never knew my parents."

Derrick pointed at my left arm, rather where my left arm once was, and he asked, "Were you born that way?"

"Oh, no," I said.

"Did you fight in the wars?"

"No," I said.

James Derrick the Sioux arched his eyebrows. His scar went from pink to white. I believe he was inviting an explanation, but I was tired, and my capacity for English had run aground.

So I nodded to Doctor Davidson and said, "He cut off my arm."

The doctor laughed and told the story. Derrick and the doctor then talked about the War of Southern Rebellion. "Never could truck with slavers," Derrick said. He and Davidson then discussed the Indian Question and battles on the frontier. The talk turned to homebuilding, for Derrick was a carpenter. My comprehension lapsed for a long while until Derrick said, "Ah, we're bound to die, and then," he said, "all questions are answered."

"It's pretty country here," said the doctor.

I didn't look out the window.

On the next morning we were barreling across a dry plain. Grey trees split upward and crows sat in the tines. Hovels appeared in the distance. Ponds opened here and there on the land. Goats were out there, wandering. We rose on a high trestle over a green, bending river, and thereafter raced around chalky hills and through trenches of stone. The land flattened out again. Round topped mountains appeared in the distance. Every so often, through the nearby brush, the white tail of a deer would dart. Throughout this time, Derrick and Doctor Davidson told each other stories. Derrick always began his tales with the phrase, "I had to laugh, once ..." and Doctor Davidson started his with "You know, they used to say ..."

Mist came in and erased all but the closest track of the plain, its spare trees and brush. Again we went through stone trenches. We came out, and the mist was gone. Beyond the plain, the mountains rose in layers. The farthest were blue and tall, and lay themselves altar-flat to the heavens.

Then the land changed once more. The trees and brush were suddenly white with frost, but only on one side, as though painted in one direction. As we raced further west, the frost crept with us, and the plain became an unending gallery of silver. The train stopped at a station without a name.

Many passengers, myself included, disembarked.

We examined an immense, frost-coated pine tree that stood by the platform. The frost, an accumulation of crystals, stood in half-inch spikes on each and every twig and needle. We marveled at these frost spikes, quills really, so tiny and articulate, and then doubly marveled how they had multiplied over the vast, arid landscape. Children ran out to chase and hide in the bright and icy brush. A line of mothers watched from along the platform. I recall a boy dancing in a taunt of his sister. He splayed his blackened fingers and hopped foot to foot. She snarled like a wildcat. They collided in a fierce embrace and ran off. An infant in the arms of a woman beside me cried, expelling steam from its shuddering, red face. She laughed and tucked its arm, which was waving free, back into the blanket swaddle. The infant's gleaming mouth went silent, overcome by the next scream.

I got down from the platform and walked out into the silver land. Coming up a ridge I spotted cows amid the frosted brush. Gusts of steam turned from their nostrils. Their warm eyes watched me. I walked further up. The sky was white at the edges and a plummeting blue above.

The world seemed to spin, and in my mind I conjured Klara. I imagined her beside me in this strange land of frost and brilliant air, her cheeks flushed, her eyes dark and gold, her throat bare.

I'll never find you, I thought. *America is endless.*

I was free and alone.

The train whistle blew, and my reverie in the crystalline expanse ended.

Twenty-five

Two days later, a train called the Pumpkinville Express brought us into the Arizona territories and to the town of Tucson. Tucson was the last place on the itinerary Renner had provided us, and so we disembarked. The station was new, and Tucson appeared small.

Wastes encircled it. The Sun stared down.

After finding a hotel, the Palace Hotel, a brick faced building, the doctor and I walked the main drag. He remarked on the architecture, the Iberian arches, the doric columns at the bank. People passed in the glare and disappeared into dark doorways. At one end of Tucson, a merciful river flowed, bringing a touch of green and trees. Children ran about. Their minders sat beneath the trees.

We stopped at the druggist. Davidson bought a tonic, drank it down in one go and made the acquaintance of the proprietor.

A woman asked us, "Are you the doctor and the one-armed giant who came in on the train?"

"I suppose we are, madam," said Davidson.

"Well, now I've seen you," the woman said. She looked at me. Her cheeks were red and her eyes pale. "And you ain't so tall," she said, "no taller than my nephew."

Davidson said to her, "We've been admiring your fine city."

"Are you foreign?" she asked.

"I am a citizen, madam, and a United States Army veteran," Davidson said, "but I am a stranger here. Have you noticed, by chance, a trio of other foreigners?"

"A trio?"

"A woman, tall and comely, dark hair; a man, a gentleman, small in stature, graceful in attire; and the third of the trio, an elderly woman. Thin."

"No," the woman responded, "I cannot say I have seen such characters."

I looked to the proprietor. He was a man with a high collar and enormous side whiskers. He flushed and sputtered, "Oh no, I have not seen this trio, either."

We thanked them for their time and took our leave back out into the Sun.

— It was then that Klara spotted us. She was sitting by a window on the second floor of Tucson's other hotel, the Hotel El Presidio. Looking down into the street, she saw me and Doctor Davidson. It was just a moment. We were two men, one short and dark suited, the other tall and with a pinned up sleeve, both of us in short brimmed hats. We crossed the bright dust of the street and into the dark doorway of a saloon.

Klara was not alone in the hotel room. She was with Nurse Kindersley and Mister Persson, and she turned to see whether they had also spotted Davidson and me. At that moment, however, both Kindersley and Persson were occupied away from the window. Nurse Kindersley was in a chair on the other side of the room and was reading from Revelation, or someplace else at the end of the Bible. Persson, meanwhile, was kneeling in the corner and praying to God. They had told Klara that I'd been hanged to death in Philadelphia.

But there I was, alive in Tucson.

The infant within her turned.

Klara stayed by the window.—

Meanwhile, Davidson and I were in the saloon opposite the druggist. There were a few men in broad hats at the bar.

I got us glasses of lager beer. Davidson sat at an angle from me, his legs crossed and his hands folded on his lap. The foam of his beer thinned.

We were both pointed towards the street and the brightness.

I finished my beer and returned the glass to the bar.

The saloon possessed a slender, fair haired young woman with her sleeves rolled up. She had freckles to her fingers and lips. I set the glass on the bar, she looked at me, and her eyes, which I believe were green, joined the shine of the daylight glancing across the brass, bottles and glasses.

"Another?" she said.

"Please."

When I returned to the table, the doctor was looking at me.

I drank my beer.

"Aren't you going to drink your beer?" I asked him.

He shook his head.

"May I?" I asked.

He nodded.

I drank it. It was a short glass. The doctor was still looking at me.

"Yes?" I said.

Davidson took off his hat and knocked the dust from it with the heel of his hand. "I am quite happy to travel and see my country, to escape the winter," he said, "but I wonder what you're doing."

I stifled a sneeze. I don't know where it came from.

"Józef," he said, "you proposed this journey, this pursuit, as a matter of great urgency."

"It is urgent," I said.

The doctor returned his hands to his lap and looked again into the brightness.

"Doctor," I said, "it's just that we are two people, and ..."

I was going to say that I had not fully imagined the vastness of the country, but in truth I had imagined the vastness, almost precisely, as though I had beheld the land from the upper spheres of the sky, and for a moment as the clarity of this fearsome vision struck me—seeing ridges, rivers, and dry expanse below me—I could not speak.

"I'm beginning to understand you Józef," the doctor said, "and how you went from a monk to a soldier, and from a soldier to a sailor to whatever you are now."

"I was a novice," I said, "not a monk."

"So, even then you stopped short," the doctor said. He stood. "I'm going back to the hotel."

He left, and after a moment, I launched out of my chair to follow him.

Klara spotted us from her window.

Perhaps the doctor and I were in the saloon for longer than I have indicated. The Sun was low now, and in the slanting light couples materialized. They strolled arm in arm. I trailed behind the doctor for the length of the town back to the Palace Hotel.

In the lobby, before the staircase, he stopped and took hold of the newel post.

"Please, Doctor Davidson," I said to him, "forgive me. I'll pay you back."

The doctor looked over at me, stricken. The lobby wall was covered with the mounted heads of antelope. They stared black-eyed from the wall.

He recovered himself.

"Oh, Józef, it's just the journey," he said, "and the Sun."

He removed his tin from his vest pocket, shuttled a few cubes into his mouth and chewed them down. "Here, take this," he said, placing a cube in my palm, "but do not neglect nourishment." He then folded a few banknotes into my hand. "Go," he said, "eat."

The doctor patted my cheek with his soft, cold hand. He turned and with effort he ascended the stairs.

I ate the morphine and departed the hotel into the last of the sunlight. I wandered the perimeter of the town like a ghost. At one side were clay hovels, and around on the other side of town were wooden homes, unfinished, showing interior staircases and rooms, as though suddenly abandoned. I turned around. Trees on a mountain's purple slope little by little folded into the darkness. I headed into town and wound up back at that saloon, which was long and narrow, and now full of noise and cowboys.

Whiskey was cheaper than beer. An Ohioan and an Englishman made my acquaintance. The Ohioan had been on the train, as well, and we toasted Derrick from Dakota, the Sioux. The Englishman took a guitar down from the wall, coaxed a tune from its neck and the Ohioan hummed, sweet and wavering. The fair haired barmaid appeared at our elbows and made a comment that broke the Englishman into hysterics. He buried his face into the crook of his arm and came up smiling, his face tight and cooking with the heat of the whiskey. She delivered another comment, this one at me, and now the Ohioan fell to laughter. I could make out only that she was Irish. She disappeared to the other end of the bar. A blonde braid ran down her back. The Englishman said to me, Boy, go get her. The Ohioan shook his head and said, She's a child. I went down the length of the saloon, walking as though upon a ship pitching forward. I passed a dozen cowboys and reached the end where I met the bartender, her father I'm sure, a barrel chested, big headed, green eyed man who leaned over the bar to hear me. Whiskey please, I said. His hand had speed, and I'd soon poured two into my stomach.

"Excuse me," I said to him, marshaling my

English, "have you seen three foreigners? One small gentleman, an old woman, and a tall woman? Foreign like me." I put my hand to my chest.

I believe he took my meaning, for he held up three fingers to confirm and then he pointed to a far table where no one was, as though to say, Yes, three such people were there, and perhaps that's precisely what he said, but I could not understand him.

I turned, the cowboys formed a tunnel, and I resurfaced back by the Ohioan and the Englishman, who were singing, but stopped when they saw me.

"You all right, Joe?" asked the Ohioan.

I did my best to explain.

"You got a woman?" he said.

Yes, I said.

"You got to go on back to her, friend!"

I could not make myself clear. I could not think.

"Listen," the Ohioan said, and he went to the following effect:

"Let us say you walk into yon street and into the hooves of a raring horse. Let us say this horse and its hooves stoves in your head. I mean you hit the ground, and your brain comes dribbling out its pan like sauce boiling over. Now, you're dying." Here, he poked me in the chest. "Who do you want by your side, looking upon you as you die, Joe? Who?"

The cowboys multiplied around us. Hard eyes, staring.

Or perhaps they were miners. Their faces were blackened.

I said to the Ohioan, "Before Klara, I knew only whores!"

"Well," said the Ohioan, "go on back to her!"

"She is gone," I said. But perhaps she wasn't.

"Do as you're told!" the Ohioan said.

"Come now, boys," said the Englishman and he led us out through the hats and hard shoulders of the cowboys and miners.

From her window, Klara then saw me in the street.

I was with the Englishman and the Ohioan. The Englishman was shouting, and the Ohioan was hanging on my arm, laughing, saying, "Oh, Joe, he took that guitar!" The Englishman had indeed taken the guitar. He was strumming a chord as he shouted in the street.

There was no mistaking me, Klara could see. Józef Nowak, seed of calamity. A tall man, perhaps a Jew, with curly hair and one arm.

The Ohioan and I followed the Englishman, who now walked with one foot in the street and the other on the wooden curb. In a turn or two, the Englishman had us seated in another saloon, one with a square bar. The sight of the barmaid took me by the throat.

She was a full and glorious woman. The Englishman and the Ohioan whispered vulgar tribute. Her dairies, they said. Her caboose, they said. And on. She served us with rough grace, thumping a thick bottomed bottle on the bar, sliding our glasses and laying our money into the till before turning away. The Ohioan was flush with color. He was young, a country boy with a block of sandy hair beneath his hat. The Englishman hung the guitar in the antlers of a mounted deer head and, taking his whiskey, backed into a darkened corner to sit at a table with an old man. The Ohioan wandered into a group of five or more men on the other side of the bar. Soon he was indistinguishable from them, telling stories, falling silent, and laughing in their rhythm. The barmaid leaned on the stretch of bar before me. She asked, "What kind of foreign are you?"

I said, "Polish."

She replied, "Never heard of you."

"We are a tyrannized people," I said.

She nodded and said, "I'm partways Apache," then added, "Have you heard of us?"

I nodded.

"Otherways I'm German," she said, resting her fist on her cocked hip.

"The German is my oppressor," I said.

"That so?" she said. "Where's your arm?"

I answered in German, "My arm is in an ash heap, or at the bottom of the sea."

She smiled, just a small sneer. "You speak your oppressor's tongue," she said.

I finished my whiskey and said, "As do you."

"English is useful," she said.

"German is glorious," I replied.

"Glorious?" she said.

"Or perhaps it's the Apache in you," I said.

She straightened up and poured me another whiskey. "How old are you?" she said. "I could be your mother."

"I'm an orphan," I said. "I've always wanted a mother."

She laughed, and in her laugh, her age showed. It showed by way of the lines around her painted eyes and mouth. It sounded from the gravel in her throat, betraying a life burning hotter each year. She then made her rounds of the bar, and in watching her, I was overwhelmed by the desire to praise. Praise her rank appeal, her loveliness so large and bound in a corset, her unnaturally black, unruly hair, her carnal dignity. She came around, polishing a glass, and smiled to see the look on my face.

"So," she said, eyeing my pinned up sleeve, "tell me what happened."

Believe it or not, there's a class of women that hunger for maimed men.

"Battle," I said.

"That so?" she asked. "Which war?"

"As a child, I fought the Southern Rebellion," I said.

"You know, this bar is full of old rebels," she said, meaning, I believe, the crew into which the young Ohioan had disappeared.

"Never could truck with slavers," I said, borrowing a phrase.

"Me neither," said she, shaking her head. "Never met men so slow to pay the bill."

I finished my drink, emptied the rest of the doctor's money onto the bar and said to her, "Meet me out back."

She swept the money into her hand, held my gaze for a long while, then said, "All right."

I went outside, but did not keep my tryst with the Apache German barmaid. Starlight had shot through the Tucson sky. It spun. I leaned against a murmuring chicken coop and relieved my bladder into the dust. Some rambling later and I stood on a hill beyond the edge of town among cacti stretching their arms to the stars and blackness above. A cold wind blew, and around me the wastes went on over rises and turned shades of silver. The foothills bolted into mountains that were black and purple in the moonshadow. Upon a mountain's peak, the Moon balanced in mad circularity. Tucson was down behind me, some buildings and lines on the hard land. From the desert came the yips and howls of wolves or coyotes.

I was facing east and thinking of the distance I had come, the forests, cities, sea and desert. I closed my eyes, and the blackness of my own gut seemed to swallow me. I fell to my knees, weeping, and said:

Lord, have mercy, my tears fall in your cup, and my sins in your ledger.

My soul longs for relief as a night watchman longs for day.

Oh, let my soul surrender!

I wept there in the cold desert until at last my desperation quieted. I then opened my eyes.

Nothing had changed, of course. Tucson, the desert and hills, the sky, stars and Moon. But a figure approached, faceless and black with edges that moved with the wind.

The figure raised its head into the moonlight. My hand went numb, my knees disappeared, my chest burned with cold air, and I recall a terrible thirst. The figure was Klara.

Her words to me were: "You're alive."

TWENTY-SIX

Klara was standing several yards down the rise from me. Her hair was loose. She wore a shawl.

I picked myself up from the ground and said, "Am I dreaming?"

"Am I?" said Klara. She stepped sideways, eyeing me. "Didn't they hang you?"

I must have been sweating, for I remember a cold wet touch across my skin.

"I'm alive," I managed to say.

Klara was yet at a distance, peering at me.

"Hold out your hand," she said.

I obeyed, and she stepped forward. Her face was unlike anything I had ever seen. Mask-like, hard, her eyes two shards of flint. She reached out and into my palm she lowered a rosary cross, Jesus Christ crucified, and around my hand she wrapped the beads. She cinched the rosary tight, gripping my only hand with both of hers, gripping the beads and cross into the muscle, bone, the knuckles, and in a whisper, she spoke Kashubian, the language of Hel, saying something like, *Save me, save me, put underfoot the devil*, several times over, all while staring into my eyes, reading me.

Tears fell from her eyes. She said, "You are Józef."

"I am," I said.

She pulled me forward, touching my face and bringing my hand beneath her shawl to press it, still bound in the rosary, against her stomach.

"Do you feel it?"

She was with child, though I understood at a lag. I was shocked at the heat pulsing through the fabric of her dress, the breadth of her stomach, firm and round, and for a moment, a spark shot through my hand. The infant within her moved, a sort of flickering.

Klara's eyes, full of tears, blazed. Her face was glowing, rather my eyes had adjusted to the moonlight. Faint freckles, I noticed with surprise, had spread across her cheeks. Her odor was different, too. I recall it rising from her body beneath the shawl, a dark and warm fume that cut through the breeze of cold sand and sage.

"The baby is not my husband's," Klara said.

I heard Langobard within me: *Thus a family man is made.*

"Is it," I said, "from me?"

"Yes," she said.

Physicians say the heart is a pump. Mine was a fire.

"I followed you to America," she said.

"Did you?" I asked.

"Yes," she said, "and fate has punished me for it."

"Are you," I asked, "with Mikkal Persson?"
She nodded.

"I thought he might marry me," she said.

"Does he think you're an angel?"

"He says I was sent by God," she said. She touched my cheek, my neck, and she smiled. "But you know better."

Her smell, that dark warmth, was in my throat. "Will you marry him?" I asked.

"I can never go home, Józef," she said. "I have nothing. Do you understand?"

My hand, yet wrapped in a rosary and pressed to her stomach, felt for the flickering life of the infant.

"Would you consider me?" I asked.

"Oh, dearest Józef," she said, "you have nothing."

"My prospects may improve."

"You are even less than you were," she said.

At her words, a pain occurred, a blunt burning at my stump, as though my arm was cut from me again. I said, "I'm more than a back and pair of hands, Miss Klara. I have a heart and mind that I may yet put to service."

She thought to embrace me, I'm sure, for her hands and arms tensed as though to bind me to her. Her black eyes still shone, and strands of her hair rose in the moonlight and breeze.

Beauty is truth, and truth inspires terror. I trembled within to see her.

"You far are more than you dream, Józef Nowak," she said, "but what good is it to me? What good is it to us?" All this time, Klara was looking into my eyes. "Do you understand?"

I was no priest or rabbi. Neither parochial, nor innocent. Klara had her future and future of the infant to think of. This is how living is done.

"Yes," I said, "I understand."

And though I'm not often gifted with clarity, I saw what needed done.

"Miss Klara," I said. "May I ask you something?"

"What's that?" she said.

"It's a cold night," I said, "may I see you safely indoors?"

Klara took my hand. We walked.

Strange. Klara and I had found each other in the abrupt wilderness at the outskirts of Tucson, Arizona. It felt like a beginning and end at once.

We came down the rise, and she whispered, "Look!"

"What?"

"A shooting star."

It was gone, but we went on with our eyes up, searching the firmament as though our destination was there. Like this we stumbled on desert roots and rock, and holding each other's hand, we nearly brought each other low. We laughed.

Soon, at the edge of Tucson, the ground went smooth. The town was asleep. We had a small distance before we'd part. We walked slowly. Klara looked up at the Moon and said, "Glorious night." Her smile, a look of prayerful astonishment, joyful and afraid at once, it was new to me. Her eyes were dark jewels and her cheeks shone, but I recall most of all a moment of moonlight on her teeth, her canines so sharp over the black of her mouth. I realized that for all my worship and pining, I had failed to be fully alert to Klara. I did not know her, and her strangeness was a brutal and thrilling blow to my chest.

We walked a ways further, our steps light, ghostly. We passed dark windows and eaves. The street was the color of the moon-brightened clouds.

Klara stopped and said, "I'm here."

She meant we had reached her hotel, Hotel El Presidio.

"Shall we sit for a spell?" she said. "I get tired these days."

There was nowhere to sit, so we sat on the wooden curb with our heels in the street.

"Come here," she said, tugging me close to her side. It was as though my arm had been cut away for her. "Take this," she said, draping her shawl across my back. She passed the edge of it into my fingers, and we pulled it tight around us. She rested her head against my shoulder and tucked her crown beneath my jaw.

"I'm sorry," I said.

"For what?"

"That you left Danzig," I said.

"Oh," she said, settling into me, "I was very lonely there."

The shawl was thin and the desert cold, but there's no warmth so magnificent as a woman with child. We talked for a while, quietly.

"What does your intuition tell you," I asked, "boy or a girl?"

"Girl," she said. "In my family, there were only girls."

I asked how many.

"We were three sisters," she said, adding, "well—yes, three," as she remembered her stillborn triplet sisters, their smell and odd look and how her father buried them at sea. "What about you," she said, "any brothers or sisters?"

How little we knew of each other. I told her that I was an orphan, or abandoned at any rate, and that I had never known a blood relative.

"Here's one," she said. She again put my hand to her belly. The infant within must have been sleeping. "Who raised you?" she asked.

"Monks," I said.

She lifted her head. Her dark eyes widened. "Are you joking?"

"No."

She searched my face anew.

"It wasn't all bad," I said.

Klara was silent for a while. She put her head back to my chest.

"May I tell you," she said, "that I'm afraid?"

Here, at last, Klara told me of the strangeness of her life:

When she was a child, she said, she would sleepwalk. She would wake up outside. Nothing could stop her. Tied hand and foot. Doors and windows nailed shut. She would yet wake up outside, sometimes far from the house, in the woods, or on the beach. Klara told me of the very first time, how elves, gnomes, or animal spirits had drawn her to the sand to watch out over the sea.

Or so it seemed to her.

Then one morning when she woke up outdoors,

her parents saw that her nightdress was on inside out. She was inspected. Her virginity was gone.

"There was a foreigner in the town's lighthouse," Klara said. "Everyone blamed him."

Her mother and father sent her away to live with her aunt, Aunt Hildegarda. Aunt Hilde knew cures and charms and rites to banish spirits and ward off the Devil. Nothing worked.

Nothing has ever worked.

"It happens still?" I asked.

"Sometimes," she said, then added: "The sleepwalking comes with dreams, but dreams that do not feel like dreams.

"They are too real," she said.

"I can never remember these dreams, but I wake up knowing ...

"I haven't the words to explain it," she said. "Think of—think of a spider web. Do you see it?"

I did.

"Think of that spider web floating on the wind. Do you see it?"

I did.

"We are in that web," she said. "It's everything to us."

For some while, my eyes had been closed. The side of my face exposed to the night air had gone numb. I was only alive, it seemed, where Klara and I were pressed against one another beneath the shawl. We were in the core of the town, yet in our ears was the locust song and wind through the brush, the wind playing on the hills and sounding higher up, like a voice. Far away, an animal cried, a lonely yowl. To me, the animal was our infant, alone and hungry in the desert.

Was this world a spider's web, a web loose on the wind?

Klara spoke, and I was pulled back into the dark heat between us, the smell of our bodies, our breath and our clothes beneath the shawl. She said: "But, Józef, you know all this. You've seen the heart."

"The heart?"

"The night we met. You told me of a heart over a hill."

"That was just a poem," I said. "I wanted you to love me."

I shook in my confession.

"You're no poet," she said. "You and I are too alike." She gripped my thigh and stilled my shaking. "I have to go," she said, and then added to dispel any confusion, "I have to go with Persson."

I took her hand. "You must do what you feel is right," I said, "for you and the child, but I must tell you that I plan to become worthy of you both. I'll make a home for you—"

Klara kissed me.

Our teeth and lips banged, we were clumsy, but the connection of our warm mouths, I swear, made a circuit of all the life coiling within us, and fool as I was, love is real, and it seemed we were high over the Hotel El Presidio and Tucson, a pattern scratched into the desert, this earthly plane.

***

And something departing reality did occur, something that in the years since I cannot explain, a shift in time, or warp of consciousness, for when the kiss broke, a dawn of white golden light was on us.

Around Tucson, birds were singing. It was morning. This is no hyperbole. It was as though Klara and I had skipped several hours of the night in one kiss.

We were on our feet before the hotel, though standing a few yards aside from where we had been sitting.

Klara's eyes were full of tears and blazing with the dawn. She took my arm. "You were there," she said, "in the heart!"

"What do you mean?" I said. My voice was weak

and my mind bewildered. "I was here with you."

"You were with them," she said, "I can smell it."

And in truth, a dizzying vapor rose from me, from my skin, the fabric of my suit, my beard, a vapor of hot metal and lye. The memory of it still stings deep in my brain. I see white. But as fierce as it was, the vapor dissipated as soon as I breathed it in. In moments it thinned to nothing.

Klara stepped back from me. I raised my arm to reach her.

"You feel it," she said, "like they've beaten you."

Klara was right. My entire body was sore, brutally tired, and I quivered.

"Klara, where was I?" I heard myself say. She was backing away, now reaching for the door of the Hotel El Presidio. "I must go," she said. "I can't be with you." She went into the hotel. Light bounced from the brass and glass panes of its doors. I stepped forward, slowly, as though weighted down by the sky above, and I caught the swing of the door against my side. I pushed into the dark lobby. "Klara," I called, my voice echoing on the tiles, "I'll have a home for us! I'll rent a room from the doctor, Doctor Davidson of Philadelphia, and I have a job, as well. I'll be a newspaperman, a reporter," I said, "at Der Philadelphia Bürger, Klara!"

Klara had already gone up the stairs.

The clerk behind the desk, a man in a tie and a vest, was looking at me through the early light. The words I had called out were Polish, of course. They meant nothing to this stranger.

Twenty-seven

That morning, I staggered down to the end of Tucson where the river ran and I collapsed onto the sharp, tough grass in the shade beneath the trees. I slept. Now and again, I opened my eyes. Further down the riverside on a stretch of flat ground, a dozen or so men were at work. They rolled out a great length of canvas, hammered stakes into the ground, erected poles and pulled on ropes, and all at once, a grand tent took form. It shone with the morning sun.

Later, I got up from the riverbank.

A religious service was on in the bright, grand tent. Inside were Indians along with whites and even a few Negroes, and they were seated all, perhaps two hundred or more, on plank benches so newly cut that the air tasted of green wood. The preacher before them was a diminutive, clean shaven old man. He wore a frilled collar and white robe that looked rather like a baptismal dress. His voice was musical, and his presence attracted such calm attention that he seemed to exist in a realm of special clarity. His eyes were sad and sparkling.

I lingered a while by the entrance. A man near me whispered and beckoned me in. I smiled an apology and went on my way.

One day when I was a boy and was feeding the chickens on the monastery farm, I realized that God had left me. Or that I had left Him. Either way it was a sudden awareness, an actual twinge behind my eyes, an understanding that I was lost and alone and had been wandering heedless for some time. Was I afraid? Was I glad? At the moment, I was simply struck. The absence of God, or the presence of His absence, if that makes any sense, so affected me that I dropped the bag of feed. The feed spilled, and the chickens went wild. I sat in the dirt and stared blindly ahead for who knows how long. Had God ever been with me? I wondered. I recall raising my eyes to the tree line beyond the field. It wasn't that day, but it was a day soon after that I fled into the woods away from the monastery, and in the years since, I have not entered back into His grace.

Perhaps I'm blind.

He might have been calling to me through that sad-eyed preacher in Tucson, and had I gone into the brightened tent, a great deal of suffering might have been avoided. But in those days I did not partake in religion.

I still do not, though I know of nothing better for the pains of the heart.

The date was January 8th, 1881.

Shortly after waking from the riverbank, I called upon my friend Jakub Davidson and found him yet in his hotel bed, spectacles on and with papers spread around him.

"Hullo!" he said and he slipped his feet from the blanket to touch down on the wooden floor. A cascade of papers followed. I picked it all up, sheets dense with the doctor's scribbles, dense with place names, hours, descriptions of the weather. Here was a shorthand of our journey.

He looked about the room. His legs, exposed below the hem of his nightshirt, were thin and white, and his feet, shuffling around on the floorboards, were boney. His toes were long and misshapen. A few of them had twisted, so that their sides had become their bottom. On spying them, a tenderness for this old man filled me. I fetched his trousers from a chair by the window.

Davidson, balancing against the edge of the bed, attempted to get a leg in. I supported his back and asked, "How are you feeling this morning, doctor?"

"I am well. I am well," he said.

"Rested?" I asked.

"Yes, I am rested," he said.

The doctor hiked the trousers to his waist and removed his nightshirt, revealing his naked torso. His skin was loose, papery, and his bones throughout his chest were visible. He donned a silk undershirt.

"I am rested," he said, "and ready."

His mouth bent into a sort of rictus smile, and he flexed his arms as would a strongman. Those arms, trembling, so sharp at the elbow, so pale. He proclaimed: "Behold the very picture of rude health!"

"Yes, doctor," I said.

He laughed and resumed his project of getting dressed, looking about for his shirtsleeves, his waistcoat and tie, all of which took several minutes. Meanwhile, we talked. I believe the doctor expressed an eagerness to sample Mexican cuisine. And he may have, I think, wondered aloud about cacti, whether they had seeds. Likely our dialogue likely took many turns, turns I here elide, though in these elisions I do a disservice to the memory of my friend, for Jakub Davidson was an exceedingly pleasant man, a great waster of time, a muser, a stroller about, a soft joker. On that morning, however, I was possessed of purpose and have little memory outside of that course. Once my friend was dressed, I handed him a note, a folded slip of paper.

The note was an acknowledgement of debt, an

"IOU" I had drawn up in the hotel lobby just before coming up, and it obliged me to a tremendous dollar amount.

"Józef," said the doctor, shaking his head, "please, I've said you needn't repay me."

"You'll get every cent," I said, "and what's more, doctor, that figure includes what I *will* owe, for I must rely on your generosity a while longer."

He stared at the IOU in his hands. "Józef," he said, "it's too great a burden."

"But, doctor, I'll have a job."

"Job? What sort of job?"

"A job back east in Philadelphia," I said. "On my return, doctor, I believe I can land a position as a reporter for Der Philadelphia Bürger. It's a German weekly. Do you know it?"

"Yes, I know it," the doctor said.

"The publisher, Emil Zörner," I said, "I've made his acquaintance."

Doctor Davidson laid the IOU on the bed. He looked at the note and the rest of his papers. He stared as though puzzled, as though someone else had tossed them all about. "Józef," he said, "you won't make a lot of money."

In truth, I had no concept of my likely income.

"I'll work hard," I said. "I'll toil like a slave to pharaoh."

Davidson gave me a sour smile. And he nodded.

A poor choice of expression on my part. My face flushed. I stammered:

"Let me explain. The amount I must borrow, in addition to what I owe, is in lieu of rent, for I hope you'll rent to me a room in your gracious home for a while longer, a room not only for me…"

Doctor Davidson seemed to rise a little. "Oh, for whom then?" he said.

Here at last I told the doctor that Klara was in Tucson, that she and I had found each other, that she was with child, and I told him of the strange incident, that in the night Klara and I lost time, skipping from the dark of the night to the light of dawn.

"An occurrence of lost time, doctor, *amisit tempore!*" I declared. "And there's more, for I ached as though I'd been hauled away and thrashed with an inch of my life! Surely," I said, "my pain is evidence of your theory, the being taken, the *advenus raptio!*"

"Wait a moment," said the doctor. While listening to my description of the night, he had taken a seat in a wooden chair. He gripped its arms and pressed himself back, but now, as if we had arrived somewhere, he loosened his bearing and looked around. "Józef, you're saying that Klara is here?"

"Yes, here in Tucson." I did not tell him that she had rejected me for Persson. "Doctor, mustn't we investigate? To see what happened in the lost time? And quickly, yes? While it's fresh?"

"Investigate?"

"Through hypnosis, doctor," I said, "to probe the mind."

"The mind, yes, well," he said, "you'll need to lie down."

We both looked to his bed. It was covered, as I've described, with his papers.

"We'll go to my room," I said.

Let me be clear. I did not yet give full credence to Doctor Davidson's theories. Certainly, I had lost time. Klara, apparently, had lost time with me. We had been sitting at night, and then were standing at dawn, moved by a distance of several feet. There had been the strange smell, the sharp fume that Klara recognized, and the sudden, brutal ache throughout my body. This is all true. But I did not yet believe I had been anywhere, and I did not hope to find, for instance, that a mysterious force had sequestered me in the night. No. My hope in investigating the incident through hypnosis with the doctor was as follows:

Whether it was angels, demons, spirits, powers unknown, a trick of the mind, or the floating heart of my poem, whatever happened in those night hours, it connected me to Klara. If I could fortify this connection, if the doctor and I could discover something of its nature, I could grab hold of it and draw Klara to me above all others. I, Józef Nowak, could be a thread in her spiderweb on the breeze, a sinew in the thigh of her life. We'd be together.

These were my thoughts as the doctor and I crossed from his room to the room across the passageway. He had rented this room for me yesterday on arrival, but given the events of the night, it had remained locked. I thus produced the key from my pocket as we neared the door. A crack of light along the frame, however, showed that it was already open.

Twenty-eight

As I pushed open the door, I knew precisely whom I would find. Perhaps his pipe smoke lingered in the passageway. Perhaps I smelled the sulfur of a match, or heard the creak of a floorboard. Maybe I long for an enemy. I found Mikkal Persson.

The small and perfect Dane was standing in the room. He wore a royal blue suit and a high, white collar. His cheeks were freshly shaven and his blond curls slicked back. "Józio!" he cried, lifting a hand as though in celebration. "You astounding Polack!"

To this day, my hatred for the man shakes me.

I strode forward into the room, grabbed Persson by his shirtfront, carried him back and whipped him against the wall and window. He was my rival. He had stolen Klara away. And this:

Just then, as he clamped his hands around my wrist, I recognized in his grip an awful familiarity! The same iron hands had, on one terrible night, pulled me into the fireroom of the Meteorite. They had held me before Dudko's knife.

Persson! Was he the second, unseen man?

Presently in the hotel room in Tucson, as he cinched my wrist, a smile of eagerness played in his slanted blue or green eyes, as though to confirm my sudden suspicion. Either way, he welcomed our mortal struggle, and in truth, so did I. Persson and I were pure and delighted in our hatred of one another. Our bond was Satanic.

I pressed his head into the window, and the pane behind him splintered into a halo. All the world was throb and light at the end of my arm. I had taken my measure and would have thrown a straight blow to drive his face through the glass. I would have smashed his unnerving beauty.

Alas, as I then remembered, I had no other arm with which to strike.

Persson laughed. Radiant tears fell from his smiling eyes. "God bless you, Józio!" he said. "God forgive you!"

Doctor Davidson had put himself between us. "Józef!" he sputtered, straining against my chest and turning crimson with the effort. "Please," he said. Fury yet crackled through my bones and skin, but I released my hold of Persson and allowed the doctor to push me back, back across the room.

"Oh, Brother Józio," Persson said, already straightening his jacket and tugging his cuffs, "your stupendous passion. It's that quality I so admire."

"You're a fiend!" I cried.

He laughed and advanced through the sunlight

of the room. "You're mistaken, my brother. We're partners, and I need your help."

"Józef, my boy," Davidson said, "let us listen."

"Doctor, he suspects evil of you," I said, "on nothing more than the base prejudice that you are a Jew."

"Oh no, not at all, good doctor," said Persson. He touched Davidson on the shoulder. "I witnessed your fine character aboard my father's ship, and besides, we have many good and clever Jews in our employ. Now, Józio," he said.

I was in a chair and trembling with rage.

"Klara, myself and the Nurse Kindersley are due south. It is a journey of immense importance. We must cross into Mexico and soon," Persson said. "I cannot overstate its urgency. But, and here's where I need you, Brother Józio, Klara says will not leave.

"She won't go," he said. He lowered himself to the patterned carpet, one knee at a time, and clasped his hands in supplication. "Our wondrous lady, she insists she won't go without you, Brother Józio."

Persson bent forward into full kowtow, hands together and forehead to the floor. At the back of his head, there was blood in his golden curls.

"Please," he said, "come with us."

And so, at Persson's instruction, I hurried across town to the Hotel El Presidio and its garden cafe. There, in a half circle of tables in a courtyard full of plants the likes of which I had never seen, giant leaves, primeval green, thorny vines, I found Klara. She was seated at a table. Her dress was a green as deep as the leaves. Her hair was pinned back and up. I approached and knelt before her. Her face drained of color and she fixed on me with a look of fear. I took her hand. It was cold.

I spoke, whispering in my best guess at Kashubian, and each word cost great effort, as though struggling free. "My love," I said, "let us escape."

Klara was not alone. Seated beside her was Nurse Kindersley, dressed in black, upright and still, so thin and tough. The nurse smiled at me. I averted my eyes.

"Józef," Klara said, her voice trembling, "will you join us in the desert?"

"Klara," I said, "please, let's you and I go back east. I'll make a life for us."

"Yes or no, Józef. Will you join us in the desert?"

"There's nothing for us in the desert. Persson is a fiend. This woman is mad."

The nurse's smile gaped wide. Her eyes stunned me; they were blue, but had no border between the iris and white, and so the blue seeped through the white and to the edges, edges of red veins, and in the centers of these strange eyes, the pupils were vanishingly small, no more than needle tips.

Perhaps my memory is demented by the evil that would later occur.

Klara dug her nails into my hand. "Józef, will you come, yes or no?"

"Yes," I said.

"Then you must know what we intend," Klara said.

The nurse then craned over the edge of the table to put her face near mine. "Sailor Nowak," she shouted. Her breath stung my nostrils, "do you know your scripture?"

"Madam," I said, "I was raised by the monastic order of Basilians. I assure you that —"

"Do you know Revelation, Chapter 12, Nowak? Did the monks teach you that?" she shouted. Her cold spittle landed on me.

I wiped my cheek with my sleeve, and with a sudden nausea, as though I were falling, the chapter flashed in my mind: There was the woman dressed in the light of the Sun, the serpent and the desert, the Holy Infant and the flood. End Times. I looked to Klara, but her face was empty. What was she thinking?

"Do you find a man in that chapter, Nowak?" the nurse shouted. "Any mention of a one-armed man? A fool? A bitched orphan?"

"Sister, stop it," Klara said.

Kindersley was quiet.

"Józef," Klara said, "you'll join us?"

Klara was the woman of the desert, the Madonna in the Sun.

This was madness.

"Yes," I said.

A bizarre scene followed. We—Doctor Davidson and I—breakfasted with Persson, Nurse Kindersley and Klara in the leafy courtyard cafe of the Hotel El Presidio. Persson and the doctor discussed, I recall, the timber trade of the Baltic and its various ports, a conversation that somehow occasioned laughter and vigorous agreement. Klara said nothing. She ate nothing. Her face remained empty and grey. She gazed at the tiled floor.

The nurse ate eggs, sucking them from her fork.

The doctor ordered a glass of dark beer, and when it arrived, he set it before Klara. "Forgive my presumption, madam," he said, "but you appear wan, sickened, which is quite common for a woman in your condition. However, this beer, which is wonderful for minerals and vitamins, may do well to ease your unquieted stomach. And behold," he said, producing a tiny brown bottle from his vest pocket, "it may be made even more healthsome. Extract of coca, madam. Quite restorative!"

Doctor Davidson unstoppered the bottle, poured the cocaine dram into the beer, and stirred the mixture with a knife from the table.

"*Et voilà!*" he said.

Klara, suddenly sweating, shielded her eyes and took the glass. She breathed deep and tilted the glass, and while she drank, Nurse Kindersley again leaned toward me. She whispered my ear:

"The physician can know but the body. The body." Here she rapped her knuckles on the table. "The body," she said and laid her hand on my leg. "Yes, the body, even the Sun!" her hot breath hissed. "The stars and mountains, yes! Even the sea, the meteors in their blessed careers! The body, all of it. And the body can but know the body, Sailor Nowak. It's a carnal knowledge. To know. *To know.* A passing acquaintance." I made to turn away, but Kindersley craned so that I could not avoid her gaze and breath. A small froth had collected at the corners of her mouth. "All man's knowing is skin against skin, Sailor Nowak," she said. "Mere rubbing!"

At this point, a hotel employee in sleeve garters

appeared. A carriage was waiting for us. Persson had attended to our luggage.

When all was ready, he fetched us, and as we passed through the lobby, a space of polished brass, dark wood, tile and mirror, the figures of Persson, the doctor, Kindersley and Klara blackened in the light before me. I felt nothing but a twist in my gut. It was regret, or fear.

I followed them into the sunlight.

The carriage was a small sort, a buggy really. The doctor appeared at my side. "Józef, Józef," he said, patting his pockets. "Have you seen my tin?"

I hadn't. The morphine was somewhere in our luggage. Persson and the driver had lashed everything to the top of the conveyance. We boarded.

Three alone in this carriage would have done well, but with the addition of the doctor and myself, the seating was painful. Our hips mashed and legs bunched up, interlocked between the benches. I was the largest person, and thus the greatest occasion of discomfort. We left Tucson, and I closed my eyes. I endeavoured to erase my thoughts with the rhythm of the hooves, the cry of carriage springs and the wind calling as it bore down over the open land. But I could not settle. My mind thrashed about. My thoughts were of

Klara's childhood in Hel, her sleepwalking and visions. I thought, as well, of Doctor Davidson's hypothesis, advenus raptio, that an unnamed force had kidnapped us. I thought of the lost time in the night prior and recalled the sharp and vanishing smell of hot metal and lye. I thought also, to my surprise, of that night months ago when the Moon jumped across the Irish Sea, and some white, winged creature, angel or albatross, appeared before the passengers of the Meteorite. But most of all, again and again, there appeared in my mind the heart over the hill, the figment of my poem. I could see it in flashes, this glowing organ. Its veins shook like lightning.

Thusly troubled, I would open my eyes. Klara was as far from me as could be in this bundle of bodies. She laid her hands across her belly and despite the jolts of the coach, she rested her head against the window. The golden land of Arizona raced in the foreground. In the distance, it turned slowly.

Hours passed. My distress was significant.

We arrived in Nogales, a border town amid hills of red earth. We passed around the town's edge to a small station, and there a train was waiting. It would take us into Mexico. The train was narrow gauge, had only two cars, and its little engine was night blue and decked with stars. Its name was El Cometa.

We climbed in. El Cometa's astronomical theme continued. The vault of the ceiling was painted with stars and planets and a comet with a long white tail. "Wonderful," said Davidson, turning in the aisle, pointing, "just wonderful. Look: accurate constellations!"

"I'm pleased you like it, doctor," said Persson.

"Oh, I do," said the doctor, and taking his place he added, "Here, I'll sit under *Canis Major*."

Rather than hard benches, the seats were small, red velvet sofas. Polished wood tables were set between them. Gold tasseled blinds hung over the windows. A green carpet ran down the aisle. The heating stove was burning fragrant wood. With these charms, I admit, El Cometa leavened the unease that had gathered in my chest. I took my seat, and as Klara passed me in the aisle, she squeezed my hand and smiled upon me. My heart opened.

Nurse Kindersley took the seat opposite me. She was wearing a black hooded bonnet. Her gaze came at me as though from a cannon.

At the moment, however, I could almost laugh.

El Cometa eased out from Nogales, and the steward, a trim, white haired man with a waxed mustache and a vested, gray suit, addressed the car.

Persson put the steward's speech into German: "He's welcoming us aboard the Comet," said Persson, "saying that if one is surprised at the opulence, one should know it bears testament to the wealth of the land.

"This was once the private train of the heir to the Sonoran Mining Trust, and it transported the heir from his lead mine in Nogales to his zinc mine in Magdalena. However, this heir made a grave error. A crime. The heir aligned himself with Napoleon III and the pretender Maximilian against Mexico. You see, the mining heir supplied lead to the French invaders of 1861.

"But by God's grace and the will of His people, Napoleon III, Maximilian, the heir and all their kind were defeated, and —"

Here Persson missed the name of Benito Juarez, the elected President of Mexico.

"— a humble man of peasant roots, an orphan, a man who had trained as a priest and who loved Mexico, who fought for Mexico, and who, once restored to power by the people of Mexico, wisely seized the holdings of the Sonoran Mining Trust. Since that seizure, the train has served the people of Sonora, and we are honored to have you with us today."

El Cometa drew near a hamlet on red hills. Children ran on the ridges above us.

The steward then gestured to the ceiling and spoke. Persson again translated:

"We commemorate here the comet that traveled westward over Cadiz, Spain, in the year 1648. The comet moved in the sky for several days and was witnessed by —"

Here Persson missed the name of Eusebio Kino, a Jesuit missionary.

"— who saved the soul of Sonora. Father Kino, an Italian and a scholar, had hoped to travel to China, and he saw the comet as a foretelling of God's Vengeance, for men have always shuddered at comets, both learned men and idiotic men."

The steward took his eyes from the ceiling and looked at us passengers.

"Does it not say in God's Holy Word that there will be signs in the Sun, Moon and stars?"

"Amen," said Nurse Kindersley from her black bonnet.

"Indeed the comet put Father Kino in mind of the world's end—"

"Amen," said the nurse.

"— The cleansing by celestial fire."

The steward then gestured to a small bronze horse and rider in a niche by the heating stove. The horse had its head bent, as though bowing to drink from a river, and the rider looked skyward. It was a statuette of Father Kino. He was wearing a cape and a broad hat and had a book, presumably the Bible, over his heart.

"When Father Kino landed in Mexico," the steward said via Persson, "which was then New Spain, the learned Italian took for his patroness the Virgin of Guadalupe."

The steward, hand still outstretched, pivoted, bringing our eyes to a Madonna. She was of plaster, or wood, and stood within a niche of rays of painted gold. Her feet rested upon a sickle moon, and she wore a blue cloak spangled with tiny stars.

As I have said, I had no Spanish, but I had retained the French and Latin of my education, and the steward went on to say—I believe—that the comet over Cadiz did not foretell the end of the world. Instead the comet was a holy demand from the Virgin Mary that Father Kino go west to the land of Sonora and bring the Word of God to the Indian.

Persson, however, breached his role as translator and instead declared:

"The Mother of God told Kino that someday into the desert would come a great man, an heir to God."

"Praise be," said Kinderley.

"And that this great man would ascend by angels to His throne."

Persson was looking over my head to the Madonna. The sunlight fell on his face. The golden tassels of the blinds danced above his head. He shut his eyes against the Sun. His teeth were glistening. A glory possessed him.

El Cometa left the hills for a plain of green brush. We gained speed.

Magdalena, our terminus, was a town of white stone along a sandy river. At one end was the mining heir's manse, which was now the town hall and garrison, and at the other end was a church and a tiled plaza ringed with lemon and orange trees. A spine of mountains made the eastern horizon. Desert, and eventually the sea, lay to the west.

We disembarked El Cometa and boarded an open wagon that took us through the heart of the town and out to an expanse of orchards. The driver was bringing us to an inn on Magdelena's outskirts, but as we rode, a bell rang.

"Go back!" Kindersley exclaimed. She was pointing. At the bottom of the yet blue sky, a bell swung in silhouette in the gable of a church tower. "A sign!" she said.

Persson directed the driver back into the town. "We shall partake in Mass!" Persson declared. "We shall, as the saint once said, 'Do as the Romans do!'"

Klara, sitting across the wagon from me, reached out and touched my knee. "Józef," she said, "will you come to the church?"

The winter Sun had brought out copper in her black hair and the freckles on her cheeks.

"I should like to ——-" I said, and it was true. However, at that moment, a singular imperative awoke within me:

Recover the *amisit tempore.*

If I could but recall what happened in Tucson in those lost hours, I might rescue Klara from Persson's and Kindersley's madness.

"— But it's been a long day," I said, "and I'd like to see the doctor settled."

Klara smiled. The wagon shook, and she cradled her belly. The green of her dress was deeper than any green of the desert. It seemed indeed she was carrying a new world.

Magdalena was small. In a matter of moments, we had reached the tree-lined plaza and its church, a white building with a blockish tower, terracotta shoulders and a dark, arched entrance. I got down and took Klara's hand.

She alighted, and as I looked to her, her face in golden light, her body pregnant, she was as she had appeared to me a year ago in a Danzig tavern: a stand of flames, the queen of my soul, the goddess of my firmament, only more brilliant and obliterating than before. A kind of happiness destroyed me. Call it love.

"Thank you, Józef," she said.

I climbed back into the wagon and took my seat. The driver spoke to his mules, and the wagon pulled away. Klara turned and followed Kindersley and Persson into the dark entrance of the church.

I would never again fully behold her.

"Could you have imagined, Józef," Doctor Davidson said, beaming, holding his hands high as we rattled down the town's strip, "that you, a boy from Bialystok, would come across the world to this marvelous place? Smell the air, Józef! What is that smell? Sagebrush? And what are those —" he said, squinting to the sky, "— condors?"

They were common gulls.

"Doctor," I said, "we have an hour."

"An hour? For what, my boy?"

"The hypnosis."

Twenty-Nine

Doctor Davidson would not discuss it further, lest we taint the process.

In short order, we reached the Hotel Magdalena. The hotel's mistress, a tiny woman, commanded us to follow her through a shadowy blue courtyard and up a flight of stairs to a collonaded balcony. She moved as though gliding. Davidson carried his valise, I carried the carpet bag, and two skinny boys, quick on our heels, carried the remainder of our party's luggage.

The doctor's room was a simple and clean chamber off of the courtyard. It had a desk and a chair, a broad mirror, a washstand with a ceramic bowl, and an arched window overlooking citrus groves that stretched towards foothills.

"*Maravillosa!*" said Davidson. He plied the boys with American coins, and they left, scurrying after the mistress, bowing and smiling.

The doctor then ordered me to lie upon the bed, boots and all, and told me to stare at the ceiling. He did not swing a pocket watch, or wave his fingers. Instead, his process of hypnosis was as follows:

"Breathe as I do," he said.

I did so. It was a slow breathing that raised and dropped my belly.

"Very good," he said. "Continue breathing."

He proceeded to count backwards from one hundred and he interspersed the count with a suggestive narration of my physical state, from scalp to toes, saying for instance, "Eighty-four, your hand is unclenched, your fingers relaxed, eighty-three ..." Meanwhile, I stared at the ceiling, which was stippled and white save for brown lines of water damage that resembled a gentle coastline of hills. On reaching zero, Davidson told me to close my eyes.

I did so and was greeted by that swirl of purple and black that so often finds us in the dark. The doctor asked me to imagine I was standing upon the deck of a ship.

He told me to walk toward the stern. On reaching the stern, he said, I would open a hatch and descend a ladder below deck. He said that with each ladder rung I was descending into deeper realms of memory.

The doctor told me to imagine walking a dark corridor.

The doctor told me to see myself as though I were outside myself.

None of this visualization came to my mind's eye. I saw no ship, no hatch and ladder, no corridor, no Nowak. Instead, as often happens when I recline with eyes closed, the ghost of my left arm began to itch. Then it throbbed. Sparks of pain rebounded from the bicep to the fingers.

I ignored it as long as I was able, but the pain was too awful, an electrical gnawing, and at last I shot up from the bed with a gasp, knocking the washstand beside the bed and nearly toppling its ceramic bowl to the floor. "Oh!" said the doctor, righting the bowl.

The room appeared brighter than before. I explained my trouble, the pain.

"We need help. My tin," said Doctor Davidson. He patted his vest pocket and looked about. "I don't have it. Józef, would you check the valise?"

The valise was atop the room's desk, and just below its latches was Davidson's tin of morphine tablets. Neither he nor I had packed the tin into the valise. Without remark, I handed the tin to the doctor. He shook out three of the cubes for himself and handed it back. I took one.

A cool breeze came through the window. It carried the fragrance of green leaves and oranges.

"Oh Józef, Józef," the doctor said. He rubbed his legs. "I envy you, your youth. Such a great fortune you have. And don't worry about the nurse and that man, Persson. No, no. I have some expertise in the matter. Believe me, my boy. I've made my trade in bizarre beliefs and have often seen them disappointed. Oh, there will be some breath holding," he said, crossing his legs and stretching out his arms, "some insistence on heaven or hell, the will of God, or somesuch, but before long, reality will settle in. And then, Józef —"

Here, the old man patted me on the knee.

"— Then it's just you and Klara and a brand new infant! Mazel tov!" He clapped his hands. "You're free as birds, and in the land of the free, or Mexico, as it were."

My face burned. An unusually bitter taste coated the root of my tongue.

I was staring at the rug by the doctor's feet. The rug was woven fronds or long grass, dyed in a pattern of diamonds within diamonds, the innermost of which were white. They vibrated against a border of red, like eyes straining to see.

The doctor was talking:

"Until then, Józef, don't worry so much. The nurse and Persson, they are zealots, but they mean no harm. You needn't believe in God on his throne to have faith in your fellow man."

I raised my eyes and pictured Klara in the church. I would have liked to have knelt beside her, to hear the priest's Latin echoing on stone, to see the cup and bread raised, and see Christ, his painted blood, and all while feel the warmth of Klara and our unborn infant on the unguarded, armless left of my body. At that moment, however, the look on Doctor Davidson's face broke me from this reverie.

His mouth was slack and his lips were turning blue.

"Doctor?" I said.

There was no fear in his expression, just a touch of confusion in his eyes.

In the next instant, he fell from the chair. It was as though a great weight pulled him from below.

I moved from the desk to where he lay, but in those two or three steps, I too was pulled down. I fell sideways into the washstand. The bowl shattered upon the floor.

I crawled forward and threw myself over Davidson. We had been poisoned. I knew it at once. I put my finger in his mouth, trying in vain to clear out what remained of the tablets. I ran my finger beneath his lips and around his gums. His mouth was small, like a child's, and it had gone cold.

I withdrew my finger. The cold was in my finger now, in the bone and traveling to my wrist. But here, I cannot discern whether my memory is true, whether I felt the whitish freeze, a swift creep up my arm, and up from my toes and legs, as well, a chill that went down my throat and ended as a burning flood through my chest, or whether I right then lost consciousness. I am certain I did not feel the strike of the floor. Rather, it was as though I tumbled into myself, that infinite nowhere.

THIRTY

They—Persson, Kindersley and Klara—found our bodies. Someone stretched a sheet over the doctor. When I came to, Persson and Kindersley were pulling Klara from me. Her hand, for a moment, lay hot on my neck. The rest of me was cold. I looked for Klara. Her face was a bright circle moving away, and I heard her cry, "He's alive!"

"Witness the demon!" Kindersley said.

A burning channel ran through me. I was vomiting horrifically. Bile and blood.

"Mother Klara," said Persson. "I've attended to morphinomaniacs before. Let me take care of him."

"I've told you," said the nurse, "leave him!"

"I will attend to him," said Persson. "He can be made well if you leave us."

Persson, a blue pillar, was standing over me. He had turned to speak, to bid Klara and the nurse from the room. His coat was unbuttoned, and it parted when he turned. Something hung in the darkness beneath his coat. An indistinct curve beneath his arm and against his vest.

I closed my hand on something smooth. It was a long shard of the broken washbowl. Persson came low over me. The darkness of his coat opened. I had no thoughts, just an understanding that I had been poisoned and that Persson meant to finish me.

Nurse Kindersley knew what I would do. She said again in a hard voice, "Witness the demon."

By then, I had plunged the washbowl shard into Persson's neck. The shard was large and white. Its lip stuck out from the side of his throat. Darkness swelled around it. Persson touched the ceramic lip and sat carefully beside me. He unbuttoned the collar of his shirt and removed it from behind his neck. It lay in his hands, already half wet with blood.

I looked for Klara. "You can't leave," I said.

Klara screamed, and something knocked me aside.

The nurse had struck me on the head with the chair or the washstand. The room tipped. Rather, I tipped. The door was open, and Kindersley and Klara were gone.

"Józio," said Persson. He burbled out that name. Blood flowed over his lips, and a soft click followed.

It was a revolver. Persson held it, steadying his hand upon his knee.

He had retrieved the pistol from under his coat. I lifted my phantom arm before my face. I didn't hear the crack of the shot, but the pistol had fired. Between us hung a thin veil of gunsmoke.

It smelled of urine and sulfur. I looked from the barrel to the wall where the bullet had gone.

A small hole, smaller around than a penny, had appeared beside the door frame.

With some urgency, I crawled. Past the door, out on the balcony, I got to my feet. The doctor was yet beneath a sheet in the room, unmolested by the fracas. Persson was crying, burbling with blood, and he touched the glazed lip of the shard in his neck, as though wondering whether to pull it out. I had no doubt that I had killed the man, and so I closed the door.

I descended the stairs to the courtyard. People hid in the blue shadows. I passed through a dark arch, a gate, and came out onto the road. A carriage passed and raised a dust cloud. Above me, pink clouds were afire and the sky was both pale and dim. Dogs barked and snarled at my advance. A stench rose from me, one of poison, sweat and fear. Roosters cried, as they do. I walked for a while, wending through streets. Magdalena was larger than I had imagined. A polka played somewhere nearby. It echoed on walls and the echo hollowed out the melody. The Moon was up. Soon, I had crossed the bridge out of the town. Dark piles smoldered in a field of dust. The smoke was foul. Dogs whirled around the piles. At length, I reached train tracks. West, I thought, Klara will go to the sea. The Sun was between two hills. Darkness swept the interceding plain. Over me the sky went green. Soon, I had wandered off of the train tracks and was among tall cacti. Some stood alone. Some stood in gangs, preposterous gangs of thirty or more. The stretches of sand between them brightened under the Moon. By the roots of bushes were holes, large around as a thumb. Snakes, I feared, were traveling beneath my feet. The night went on, I kept walking, and morning came, rolling the stars back over the mountains. The cacti seemed to wake up and watch me pass between them. Dark creatures bobbed behind cacti, watching me as well. They were vultures. Later, when the Sun was bright, I realized that I should have followed the riverbed out of Magdalena. The day passed, as did the night, and the morning came again. I awoke and saw a train quietly gliding along the horizon. I hadn't wandered so far from the tracks. I got up and walked a while longer, and at some point I stopped.

With a map before me now, I reckon that I traversed one hundred miles southwest in less than three days, Magdalena to Libertad, a town near the Sea of Cortez. I remember facing the sky. Dogs, or coyotes or wolves, jabbed my face and ribs with their toothy snouts. The smell of rotting fish was in their fur. Over me passed birds, white gulls screeching and riding the drafts, and the occasional pelican, a far stranger thing. I sat up. The dogs, coyotes or wolves backed away and formed a circle of eyes, a wheel of canine attention. Night arrived. The creatures looked to the sky. Fireworks, pink and green, were launched from Libertad.

I was arrested and was brought to a third town. I'll leave the particulars to your imagination. I lay upon the cot of a jail cell and watched the stars shift between the bars of the window. Over the next week, I regained my wits and health. The jailers were patient. One had stiff, silver hair and a large mole that interrupted the right side of his mustache. His torso had the shape of a barrel. He introduced himself as Don Jaime. The other jailer was far younger, a lithe man with long hair. His name was Ivan.

Occasionally, I shared the cell with a drunk named Alejandro. He had twisted hands and but a few teeth. His tongue slipped out of his mouth when he spoke. Alejandro had a passion for military history.

One day some manner of policeman or soldier arrived to question me. He spoke excellent German. I told him that Doctor Davidson, Persson and I were missionaries and that we had come in search of Indians unredeemed in the desert. Persson went mad, I said, and he poisoned the doctor and me, as evidenced by the doctor's corpse in Magdalena. I defended myself, I said.

The policeman or soldier was beset with a permanent look of shock: large round nostrils, wide and dark eyes, an open mouth. His jacket, which was white with epaulets, was oversized and stiff, as if holding him upright.

"Did he shoot at you?" he asked.

"Yes, sir," I said.

"I see," he said. "And what kind of missionary are you?"

"I'm a penitent in the cult of the Black Madonna."

He nodded and wrote everything down. He was very young and obviously far from home. "Someone else will be along," he said.

One night when I was alone in the cell, the dogs of the town began to howl. The howls gave way to snarls and barks, echoing through the streets. One could hear the seizure of their throats, the quality of their voice. Their cries grew louder. The point of their attention was nearing. I realized that a figure was coming down the street, approaching the jail. I waited, looking at the Moon. The Moon was precisely between the bars. Footfalls neared and two hands latched onto the bars.

The figure pulled himself up. His crown was bald and his hair was white, though the Moon colored it blue. His face was obscured, and from it I could discern no features. For a moment, I took him for a dream.

"Is that you, Nowak?" he said.

I stood at the center of the cell.

"Yes," I said.

Had my eyes a moment longer to stare, to adjust to the shadow dwelling on his face, I would have recognized him as Martens, the carpenter of the Meteorite and man who had brought me to the Holy Ghost. But just then he dropped from the window.

Idiotically, I leapt up and down, trying to see him. Then I stood upon my cot and, after a few moments, I spied him in the moonlight, walking away down the center of the street. His white hair was bright upon his back and shoulders. He had a hitch in his stride and a bend in his back, but he moved fast and light. The dogs, snarling, ran at him. They danced around him, raising dust in the moonlight. But the man kept on. At some point, the dogs stopped in their tracks and barked at him as he disappeared down the street.

The dogs barked, it seemed, for hours, filling

the night air with cold echoes, again revealing the jolt of their throats, the shock, the yelp of fear beneath every utterance, a chorus of bodies. Not so long after, the Sun rose. I stood again on the cot. Now the blown dust was lit by a fiery dawn, and a single, quiet dog stood silhouetted in that dust, framed by a dark tree that reached over the road.

One afternoon the cell door opened and Don Jaime, the jailer with the stiff silver hair, beckoned me out. Let's go, Mister Nowak, he said. He led me across a courtyard and to the street. There the other jailer, Ivan, stood with two horses. I had learned a day or two before that Ivan was Jaime's nephew. The resemblance of their features was powerful, and in beholding both Ivan, a young man of honeyed skin, slender limbs and shining black hair, and Don Jaime, a gray man of rigid posture, I began to weep.

The two of them looked at me with a start, assuming perhaps that I was mad and would cause trouble.

I was awake in a way I had never been. Ivan and Don Jaime, nephew and uncle, were going to walk me into the desert and shoot me through the head. So I imagined. I did not for an instant think of Klara. Rather, I thought of Don Jaime and how he would grow older and eventually die, and how Ivan would grow older, looking ever more like his uncle, and then one day Ivan would die.

Don Jaime pointed to one of the horses, the golden sort they call a Palomino, and he gave me an order.

I tried to climb up, but eventually both men had to push me from below before I could mount the animal. Don Jaime mounted the other, a piebald pony, and he led me away from Ivan and the jail. I nodded goodbye to Ivan, but he did not respond.

Several months had passed, it was summer now, and the Sun weighed on us as though standing on our spines. The air was thick with the smell of burning sugar. The shops on the town's avenue were closed. A broadside with the image of a man's head was pasted along the walls, repeating. He might have been a touring magician, or a politician.

The town was small, and so passage into the desert took but a minute. People stood in darkened doorways. They glanced at us. Don Jaime turned and turned again, as though leading us in an outward spiral, until we came to a road that headed straight for a lone mountain.

It was sheer rock at the peak and folds of earth at the base. Someone had arranged white stones on the mountain's skirt to read: *El Rey Cristo viene otra vez.* Christ the King will come once more. Further up, someone had painted the Virgin Mary on a rock face. Still, I had no thoughts of Klara.

Don Jaime signaled me to get down. From his saddle, he placed a tattered straw hat on my head. Our merciful Lord has yet to light the ovens, Don Jaime said, but still, you're a pale and sensitive man. He gave me a loaf of bread and a skin of water.

Walk, he said.

I headed down what remained of the dusty road and stepped into the wilderness. Don Jaime followed behind, slowing as he went, and he spoke: José, do you understand me?

His voice was barely distinguishable from the breath of the horses.

Yes, I said.

Keep that mountain in front of you, he said, until it is behind you, then keep it at your back. Never come back to Mexico. He swore an oath I could not understand and added, José Nowak, at the very least, get the devil out of Sonora.

I stopped, tempted to see my jailer one last time, but before I could turn, the mountain rang with his words.

Don't look back, he shouted.

I'm going to watch you disappear.

THIRTY-ONE

In the following months I rambled and starved my way north and east. At Laredo, Texas, I got a job shoveling guano, batshit, that is. At night, I wrote a summary of my travels. I sent the little epic to Zörner at Der Philadelphia Bürger. He wrote back, saying that the story was too confusing, but further said that should I ever darken his door on 22nd Street, he'd make a reporter of me. I appeared there one day, a wretch, and he took me in. I gave Der Bürger the next thirteen years of my life. Each year our circulation declined. Die Republik, the city's more established German newspaper, poached our reporters. To supplement income, Zörner and I translated penny dreadfuls. I wrote and published *Olaf Twist* and *David Kupferfeld* and other knockoffs. Our steadiest supplement was a German copy of the U.S. Constitution. Zörner allowed me a run of Polish copies, but sales never progressed. Of course, Pepi, he'd say, a nickname he used to needle me, your people are illiterates. What about Copernicus, I'd say. What about Kepler, he'd reply. I'd say Chopin. He'd say Beethoven. And on. Please, I'd say, anything that anyone likes about Germany came from the Poles. Beer, cheese, and sausage, primarily. The Poles, he'd say, should thank us for deigning to rule them. Otherwise, you'd be Russians. Occasionally our differences became severe. But as we put in order the words of a story—I recall a landlord in Devil's Pocket dispossessing Negroes en masse; a rash of astronomical saloon tabs run up by ward-leaders; the mayor's gambling debts over staged rat fights— our minds glowed like embers of the same fire. I loved when he would edit me aloud, turning each phrase toward his long, acrobatic style, reading it back, again and again, while waving one hand in the air in the manner of an orchestral conductor. Better, no? he'd say. Yes, chief, I'd say. A little better. Zörner and I had conversations that lasted years, the sort comrades may have when they are both at task and without cause to bring the topic to a close. Zörner would drop to a murmur and confide in me the difficulty of his recent bowel movements. His digestive tract was a malevolent peasantry in the nation of his body. I knew the miseries of his physician-directed diet. He would incant his recipe for spaetzle, which he was forbidden. (I told him spaetzle was Polish). I knew the names of the ghost children that haunted his house. I knew his misgivings with his parish priest's affinity for the Irish. I knew the order of his daily prayer regime, a chain of syllables imprinted on his mind as a boy. Each week, he would say, Come with me to Mass, Pepi, and confess your sins. You embarrass good Poles everywhere. I loved Zörner, and could not help but relay to him over the years the story of my life. According to him, my childhood was a paradise. What I wouldn't have given to have been a bastard orphan in a monastery, he'd say. To him, my time as a patriot for Poland was stupidity, a disgrace saved only by the fact of its failure. On hearing of Klara, he'd bless himself and say, You were lucky to survive. Oh, come now, I'd say. He'd give me a look of feigned shock. Pepi, that woman was possessed. Here, I would retreat into myself. Zörner would advance. Once, for evidence, he grabbed my empty sleeve. She was a knife in Satan's fist, he said. He feared that she would come for me. Over the years, he had learned to peer into my eyes and see the flame Klara had left within me.

In solitude, I warmed myself by that flame. I loved her still, if *love* is the right word. I visited tall whores with dark hair. I kept presentable company, as well. In the years since Mexico, I courted two women. Both short and fair. I considered proposing marriage. These women, whom I'll save the ignominy of being named, had good character and intelligence. I was fortunate to be in their company. To them I appeared a regular man. A bachelor. A soldier turned sailor turned journalist.

And in truth I am a regular man.

I have not spent these years pining for a woman.

I have not dreamt of the child.

Yet:

Late one afternoon, the telephone in our office rang and I answered. The operator put through a call, and a man's voice squawked from the horn: "Is that you, Nowak?"

I flinched. The party on the other end was an old man, and like all old men with a telephone, he was shouting.

"Yes," I said, "this is Józef Nowak."

"Would you like to see Klara Glockner of Hel?"

He was speaking Polish, oddly accented.

"Who is this?"

"She's on the next Cunard to Danzig," he said, and with that, the line cut.

I left the office.

At Dock and Water streets, fishmongers were sweeping beneath the long eaves of the market. A cart horse idled, its head low. Further down, the public landing for Cunard steamships was empty. Just a gate that overlooked the river. Beside it was the Cunard pier, a sort of freight house that stood on stilts over the water. The ticket office rose against the street with a facade like a temple. On its roof, a man was lowering flags from their poles.

I waited a moment, pierced by my own senses.

The city was at its violet hour, and the sky was forming a dark band over New Jersey. The Delaware's water turned black and electric. The warehouses of Camden appeared as lost, hooded figures, staring over the divide. The Sun drowned beneath the western roofs, and from the river came a breeze of pure stench and ozone. Something broke within me as though made of glass, and I remembered what it was to be with Klara.

She dwelled where the veil of the world was thin.

I was upright, on my feet. Just a man lingering by the docks. Oh, but the quaking within was awful. The divine spasm! These stabbings from beyond! Could I suffer so?

I crossed the road to the ticket office.

Afterward, I returned to Der Bürger and stepped in from the street. Zörner stood in his shirtsleeves and print apron. Tomorrow's broadsheet proof was taut between his ink-stained hands and, by the light of a desk lamp, he squinted at it. "Józef," he said absently, "I've finished your story. It's too late for corrections."

From the back room came the clack-and-whir

of the press. Old Dagobert, our printer, was in that far doorway, his bald head swaying with his work.

"Has anyone been to see me, chief?" I asked.

"Since you left? An hour ago?" he said. "No."

"I see."

Zörner put the sheet down and stared at me. His face was tinted green from his eyeshade. The whole of that little office, its desks and lamps and piles of paper all askew, the yellowed walls and ceiling, the windows purpling to black with the end of the day, the smell of the ink, paper in bulk and burning oil, the rhythmic clatter of the press, it all lent strength to the stare of Zörner.

I owed him everything.

"What's this all about?" he said.

I did not answer.

"What are you keeping in your coat?"

He held out his hand. It was broad, paw-like and colored with years of cheap ink, yet his fingers tapered to clean nails. His arm had a blonde down.

I passed the ticket from my pocket to his hand. He tilted the ticket to the lamp's light and read it in a squint down the end of his nose. He then folded it, picked up his coat from the back of his chair, slipped his great arms into the sleeves, and passed the ticket into a pocket within his coat.

"Walk me home, Pepi," he said, dropping his visor to the desk.

"Chief," I said, "the ticket, please."

He shook his head. "You brought it here so that I could take it from you."

He was right, perhaps, and yet an urge nearly overcame me. I envisioned pinching him by the throat and driving his bulk down into the floor. Evidently, the rage showed. He placed a hand on my shoulder, saying, "Sit. Let's talk."

I sat in his chair, a first in our considerable time together, and he lowered himself onto a stool. As he sat, he heaved his deformed and bracketed leg out to the side. The iron and leather brace squeaked. He couldn't maintain this lopsided perch for long. The coming lecture would be quick. To get my ticket back, I just had to wait.

"Have I ever told you, Józef," he said, "of my father's dream for me?"

For every point Zörner wished to make, he had a story from the early chapters of his life. I'd heard many of them and guessed that he was about to tell me of his failed bid in the seminary, the climax of the tale being when the Archbishop of Some-Such poked young Zörner's breast and said, You cannot be a priest! Your corpulence would disgrace the church! Zörner would demonstrate the pain by poking *me* in the chest. "Your father wanted you to be a priest," I said. "You went to the seminary and studied your heart out, but the Archbishop showed up —"

"Oh no, no," said Zörner, shaking his head. "A priest? My father wanted nothing of the sort. In fact, I went to the seminary to escape my father." Zörner stared at me, perhaps awaiting another guess. Was this to be a new tale?

"Józef, he wanted me to be an opera singer."

He leaned forward on the stool, pressing his fists into his thighs.

I searched my mind for some mention of this opera business. With dread I drew a blank. "Opera singer," I said. "Why's that."

Zörner inclined his head to the ceiling and squinted. Already, I had taken a serious misstep by causing him to ruminate on his father's motivations, which unearthed a yet deeper story of his father, who as a boy, Zörner then told me, once pressed his ear to the alley door of a concert hall in Munich. A tenor emerged, Von So-and-So, a giant bathed in light and wearing a cape. The tale went on, and I entered a disembodied state, a talent and tactic I employed in my youth in the monastery, wherein all sight flattens into colored shapes and all sounds occur at a distance. In this state, time would fold, passing quickly. As he spoke, Zörner's face loomed large and his body drifted. It was working. Minutes were rocking by, until Dagobert broke the spell.

With coat and hat on, Dagobert passed behind Zörner and then snapped to attention. "Good night, gentlemen," Dagobert cried. "May the truth survive."

He turned and went out the door. The printing was done. What time was it?

Zörner resumed his tale, describing a scene of operatic exercise:

"My father would stand me at the edge of the forest and whip me to shout louder and louder. To the point of unconsciousness!"

Oddly and all of a sudden, that was how I felt. I was young Zörner, a fat little boy emptying his lungs into the dark of the woods. The image stuck in my mind, and though Zörner went on talking, I heard nothing, until once again we were interrupted.

Mister Bloodwell, our delivery man, rapped on the glass of the office door. It was very late. Zörner beckoned in Bloodwell and his two sons. Bloodwell was red-haired and saucer-eyed, and his boys, both about thirteen years old, were red-haired and saucer-eyed.

Zörner was on his feet, going over some matter of billing with Bloodwell, while the boys David and Charlie headed for the back. I accompanied them to the bundled stacks Dagobert had left. They gathered into their arms a bundle each, and I snagged a third by the knot and carried it through the office and out onto the street, following them to their blinkered nag in the light that fell from the office windows. It was mid-September and a large Moon hid somewhere behind the city roofs. The air was both warm and cold. The stone of the street yet clutched the heat of the dying summer.

I swung the bundled stack from my fingers up onto the cart where David or Charlie—I didn't know the difference—caught it. They both stood up there, blackened against the radiant night sky.

"Busy evening, boys?" I said.

"No busier than normal," said one.

Bloodwell came out with three bundles and his boys hopped to take them. After a few more trips, Bloodwell locked the gate of the cart.

"These boys are marvels, Mister Bloodwell," I said.

The boys looked at their father and then at me, their saucer eyes catching the barest glow of moonlight. Bloodwell nodded, and after a pleasantry or two, he climbed up and took the reigns of the nag. As Bloodwell's sons took their place beside him, my life changed for the second time that night.

Suddenly, I was a father.

Not only would I find Klara—I thought—but also the child.

Whether I was the true father couldn't have mattered less.

Bloodwell's cart had disappeared from the street. I opened the door of the office, where Zörner, now with a hat on, was once again squinting at the proof sheet.

"Come on, chief," I said to him, "I'll escort you home."

He laid down the sheet, extinguished one lamp and then another and came through the pitch black. His massive form emerged onto the sidewalk. He fished his ring of keys from his pocket. I told him, "Not another word about your adventures in opera, Mister Zörner. You will hand over my ticket, or I shall thrash you, one-armed or no."

Locking the door, he peered over his shoulder and muttered, "No need for threats."

We walked at his heavy yet brisk pace. The cane helped. After several blocks of quiet, with nothing but the knock of his cane and creak of his brace, and in the distance, wheels, voices and doors playing through the darkened streets, Zörner said, "I do not presume to tell you anything, Józef."

He produced the ticket from his pocket. I took it. We were at his corner. His street was a lane with small, joined-up houses and stunted trees crowding over the slate path down its middle. At the far end, he lived with his wife.

He tapped me on the leg with his cane. "Remember, Józef," he said, "you are a miracle of God."

I knew what he meant, but not what he wanted me to know. Or vice versa.

Perhaps he read the confusion in my silence, for he looked up and down the street as though someone else might happen by and make it plain to me. He sighed, touched my shoulder one last time, and turned and went down the lane, creaking and knocking, though slower now. At the far end, his bulk melded into the darkness.

THIRTY-TWO

The Cunard to Danzig would launch in a few days, a few woozy days with little sleep. Each time I woke, my room formed from a field of dark stars in my eyes. I emptied it of possessions. My miasma, a thick and lonely air that I shared with a brown mouse and many cockroaches, turned expectant, like the fume from a lit fuse. I walked the city, settling affairs, and my mind became unreliable. Where, for one, did all of these children come from? The street had suddenly filled with children running, children screaming, children staring at nothing. They walked around in small shoes, and with tiny fingers they ate rolls and fruit. They considered shop windows. They carried on a ludicrous pantomime of adult life. Far stranger, I saw Klara several times. Rather I saw women of Klara's height and darkness approaching within the crowds of the city, or in my periphery on a street corner. My breath grew short. The air simmered on my skin. And my heart would disappear from its nook in my chest and assume a massive, immaterial realm, like a cloud of gas. Through it, these women would cut. I fixed each one in my stare.

I frightened these women. A one-armed man of

great height was before them, his legs braced and his eyes blown open.

(Here, I beg their pardon.)

A body cannot go on in such a state. I fell across my bed, which was already stripped of linens. This was my last night of sleep on the American Continent, and when I awoke, hot daylight was marching through the window. I flew up from the mattress, frightened that I had missed the launch.

I arrived at the pier some hours early. I sat in the corner of a dockside cafe and watched people swarm by the windows. Perversely, the night's rest had deepened my exhaustion. I drank one strong coffee after another, but sleepiness closed over me, and my head settled in my hand, and my eyes closed, and when I opened them, the customers had turned over. Before: European elegants with cufflinks shining. Now: loose-mannered Americans in flair-legged trousers. I paid the bill, went outside, but from that gallon of coffee, I had painful need for a privy. I ducked into a saloon, went out back, relieved myself, and on coming back through, I saw by the wall's timepiece that an hour remained. I decided a beer and whisky would soothe my nerves. I sat by the window in the Sun with my drinks. The heat was too much. Also, the alcohol. Discreetly, I slapped myself. From the far end of the bar came a constant issue of tobacco smoke and—I realized at a lag of several minutes—my mother tongue. The men at the bar were Poles!

They numbered eight. Bright eyes, round heads and broad shoulders. Tears filled my eyes and native syllables warmed my mouth. It was time.

I grabbed my bag and went out.

The Cunard to Danzig was a black-hulled steamship the length of a city block. Along the pier, a crowd swelled, and in a crowd, a tall man is hated. Bags and shoulders closed around my chest. My neighbors cursed my every step. Seagulls hovered, screeching. Ships' horns called. Stewards let loose in German and English, Tickets please, tickets please. Ticket holders called back in fury restrained, Where's the queue? Is this the queue? The Sun had reached the lower half of the sky and leveled its light across our faces. The bodies, exhaustion, coffee and alcohol put me in a mean sweat, and the bitter sediment of my character floated to the surface. All the loving goodbyes and tears made me shudder. People kissed each other and then pushed me. I had bile in my teeth. The gangway was clear. I made for it. A steward put up his hand. This gangway was for first class, he told me. The short people of the world continued their revenge against my ankles and ribs. The gangway for steerage was several yards away, but as I had no one to bid goodbye to, I slipped to the front of the crowd. Then I remembered:

Klara. She was tall!

I cast about to spot her above the crowd. I appeared, I'm sure, like a frightened horse. Suddenly, round heads proliferated before me. The Poles from the saloon. They belted me with flat stares and prodded me with their fingers. They were a menacing lot. Every last one had pale eyes. "Chozdmy, chudy," said one. *Let's go, string bean.*

I strode up the gangway to a door opening into the hull. A steward examined my ticket and gently pushed me into the cool corridors of the ship. I ignored the brass plaque pointing the way to steerage and instead went up a staircase, searching for a vantage point. A steward called after me. I kept going.

The sheer space within a ship always thrills me. Each one is a brazen secret.

The corridors were a maze, hallways of polished doors and long, red rugs. I passed through a restaurant where waiters were spreading red-checked tablecloths. Another level higher had a small casino with slumbering tables of craps and roulette. There was a saloon full of sunlight. I made it outside. First class passengers were already promenading the main deck with sun umbrellas. White jacketed waiters wove between them with silver trays bearing bright flutes of champagne. I was distressingly high above the pier, but from the railing I could make out the passengers heading up the gangways. I looked for Klara in the crowd. I looked for the child.

I'm not such a ragged customer, but it wasn't long before a steward asked to see my ticket. He was a squat man. He turned my ticket over twice and said, "Come with me, sir." I followed him and his white cap down staircases and into steerage. Steerage looked like a hospital ward. It smelled of ammonia. We crossed the families' section. They were few. The children were very young. The bachelors' section was wisely separated from the families by a luggage keep. The men that had settled were opening bottles. Others were ducking and squinting, looking for their bunks. Lo, upon my bed was one of the Poles. For a moment he acted as though I wasn't there, but then climbed to the top bunk and offered me a drink from his bottle. Bathtub vodka. It lit up my throat and belly.

He peered over the edge. His eyes glittered. A young man, eighteen, give or take. "Heading back, mister?" he asked in Polish.

"Indeed," I said.

Soon I was in with their lot, talking about American work and Polish hometowns. Talk of women occurred, as it does, and I took it as a signal to resume my search for Klara and the child.

I scanned the families and stood by the entrance to the ladies section toward the rear. I searched the open-air stern deck, and saw nothing but pigeons on the railing. Inside, I stepped over a few brocaded ropes and was soon through the corridors of second and first class, the restaurant, casino and saloon. These places were coming to life. Perhaps Klara had come into money and now mixed with our betters. The squat, white-capped steward spotted me again. Soon back at my berth, I drank with my countrymen and grew ever more fueled and warm. I told them about Klara.

"You'll find her, Józek!" they cheered. So I left. On my return with the steward once more, they cried, "Poor Józio!"

Camaraderie spread with bottles passed, games of cards played on suitcases, and dice on the floor between the bunks. We Poles turned to the non-Poles—mostly Danes, Germans and Irish—and hammered out conversations in American English, nailing slang from Wyoming to Maine. Some of us took on a Northern European mélange. Our words landed in soft nests. All together, the smoke, the flatulence, and the reek of our armpits, mouths, wool and booze replaced the ammoniac air. "I'm not such a fool," I told a man who sat on the bunk next to mine. "I know she's on the ship," I said. "I can feel it."

The ship was spinning. I was a little drunk. I opened my eyes and saw Martens.

He'd become an ancient man with a mottled, hairless head. He wore a black suit with a red tie. Around his eyes spread deep creases, and his eyes within them were glimmering, black lines. He nodded and smiled at me, a knowing gesture. On his lap sat a narrow, black box.

I did not recognize him. The box was the same dark tone as his suit. It made no impression.

I got up and went to take the air on the stern deck and to say goodbye to America.

Before long, Martens joined me. "Here you are," he said, "tempting the angels, are we?"

I said nothing.

My spirit was at odds with the idyll taking shape along the river. Seagulls gathered on the Delaware, white breasts to the water. The wind drove dark, rippling lines. The Cunard was leaving a glassy field in its wake. The Sun was deep red and settling into a forest on the horizon, and on the other side of the sky, the Moon hung low in the blue darkness over the water. My heart was a bloody fog in my chest, a poison.

"Does it still happen?" Martens asked. He was speaking Polish, though in a strange accent, meaning that he was one of the few people who had learned our tongue outside of childhood. This earned him a glance from me. He had the black box belted to his chest.

"You've confused me with someone else," I said.

"You're Józef Nowak," he said, "former stoker of the Meteorite and disciple of Mother Klara."

Have you noticed that when someone has you at a disadvantage, when they recognize you, but you do not recognize them, that in that moment that person possesses a gravity superior to yours? You fade a little, as though drifting. This sensation must have played on my features, for Martens lifted his hands and clarified: "You would know me as Martens, the carpenter of the Meteorite."

By his black eyes, which glistened like tips of melting ice, I recalled him.

"I call myself *Ligvogler* now," he said.

He had retained his apish and starved look, yet was wholly different. It wasn't simply that his hair was gone, or that he was older, or that he wore a fine, black suit. Rather, it's that he was free of menace. He'd become a harmless and tidy old man.

"Ligvogler, in my language," he said as if to dispel my confusion, "means follower of the light."

Ligvolger. Martens. My mind couldn't yet close the gap.

"I've left carpentry behind to spread the good word," he said.

"How original," I said.

He smiled, and I noticed again the narrow box belted to his chest. It must, I reasoned, contain valuables that he thought better than to leave unattended. Not such a strange thing, but under the circumstances, in which I was suffering from an oversupply of mystery, I couldn't bear the sight of it.

The sky was devoid of daylight, and the stars, as though party to this man's designs, had suddenly appeared. For years I had been in the city, under its nights of haze and smoke, and so the stars shocked me. To my eyes, they were mad with brightness and far too close to our Earth.

"Tell me," he said, taking hold of the railing and looking to the sky as well, "when they take you, how much of it can you recall?"

"What do you mean?"

"The angels," he said, "when they carry you away into their—what's the word—their *communion* with God."

"I haven't the faintest fucking clue what you're talking about," I said.

He smiled. "We share so much in common, Józef," he said. "We ought to be honest with each other, no?"

Then it struck me: "Martens," I said. "It was you on the telephone."

"I'm guiding you," he said, and he gestured to the bay, "as a fellow disciple."

"Where is Klara?"

"She is lost, like you," he said, now gesturing to the dark land of Pennsylvania.

"The child," I said. "Where is my child?"

"Oh," he said, "the child is here, on the ship and safe."

"Where?"

"You must recall, Józef, that night on the North Sea," he said, "when you were near the bow of the Meteorite, on a break from the fire room," he said, "and lightning struck you."

"Lightning? What are you talking about?"

He raised a hand to heaven. "The sky was clear. Then lightning! But," he said, looking to me and taking hold of my shoulder—the box brushed against me—"do you recall that the lightning made no sound?"

"No," I said. This madman had lured me onto a ship. "Where's my child?"

What had I done? I had surrendered shelter of roofs, street lamps, smoke and stench, the steeples, the noise, trams, horses, people, work, and filth, these things that keep the heavens at bay. Oh, Philadelphia, save me from God! But Philadelphia and its trail of towns had long since darkened into shapes and disappeared as lights around a bend in the river. Soon, deeper in the night, we'd round Cape May, the southern tip of New Jersey, its last tooth of land, and the ocean would begin with all the radiance of a mortuary slab. We'd lie prone upon its imbecilic infinity. All the stars and their pricks upon us.

"You needn't hide the truth from me," said Ligvogler.

"I swear on my grave that I don't know what you are talking about," I said.

The air, despite the breeze, was boggy and sulfurous, and whether by vodka, by the motion of the sea reaching us in the bay, or by Ligvogler's disorienting presence, I felt I would vomit.

"Is she dead?" I asked.

"No!" he said, gripping my arm. The box strapped to his chest was now against my sternum.

"She's lost, but will return," he said. "Have faith, Józef."

"Is my child dead?"

"Your child?" he said.

"Yes," I said.

Ligvogler looked around. A few other people were on the stern deck. One man was trying to light his pipe. At the far curve of the railing a couple watched the Moon. Music played from the upper decks. "Perhaps we should go under," said Ligvogler.

THIRTY-THREE

We sat on a bench below deck in the curve of the aft walls. Nearby, the propeller turned in the bay, and all around us the ship's iron sang a low song.

Ligvogler began working at a buckle under his jacket, loosening the strap. He shifted and worked at a second strap. The box parted a few inches from his chest.

"Here," he said, handing me a small book. "That might interest you as a newspaperman."

I opened it. News clippings were folded within, affixed to the pages. The first clipping had yellowed, and the ink had faded. The light in the passageway was dim. At some paces was a dying lamp, riveted to the wall. Still, I made out a bit of the headline. It was in Spanish. *Santo niño*, it said. Holy child.

Ligvogler settled the box across his lap. In the moment before he raised the lid, I knew that it was a coffin, and that it held my child.

"Oh," I said, looking down upon the precious thing, "my God."

The child was no bigger than my hand. It was partly rotted and was dressed in white silk and lace.

"I have preserved it as best I'm able," said Ligvogler.

Its eyes were enormous for its size, but were sealed beneath eyelids of deep bruise blue, eyelids that had no seam, no way to open and allow sight.

The mouth was a tiny slit without lips. And the skin around the opening had drawn tight. It pulled on the tiny chin bone and the makings of a jaw. At one cheek, the skin had thinned to a patch of nothing, a cavity into the head.

The infant was an oddity, deformed. It had no nose, not even the slightest bridge, but only nostrils, tiny openings.

"I emptied the blood," said Ligvogler. He produced a vile of dark liquid.

"The blood?" I said.

"Yes. The veins have arsenic now," he said, "for preservation."

Perhaps the arsenic accounted for the strange smell rising from the little body. It was like garlic weed, or old onions. Sharp and sweet and sickening.

The veins of the poor creature showed; from the cheeks to across the temples and up the sides of its bare head, they stood out as hardened rivulets. The child had no ears.

In my youth, I lived among skulls, dozens and dozens in the monastery, including those of babes, and the shape of this child's head was unlike them all. This poor creature had suffered hydrocephalus, I reasoned, that watery ballooning of the head.

Its hands, which were laid across its chest, were minute, more delicate than the lace cuffs of the silken sleeves. Ligvogler had arranged in the grip of its tiny fingers a dried flower.

"The Holy Infant requires much tending," said Ligvogler, and he took from his pocket a small case and opened it. Inside was a set of brushes. He produced a little jar and unscrewed the cap. He dipped a brush into the jar, which contained a sort of varnish. He then painted the infant's cheek, or rather he painted around the hole in the infant's cheek. He scarcely touched the brush's tip to the skin. The varnish left a sheen. He dipped the brush once more and painted around the infant's lipless mouth. I shuddered, afraid the brush would reveal the child's teeth.

"Is it a boy or a girl?" I asked.

Ligvogler leaned close to its face, inspecting his work. "It is neither," he said in a breath. "It's a creature of the heavens."

He drew back and screwed the lid on the tiny jar in his hand.

"It's brought me great joy, and a bit of money," he said. "I've exhibited this blessed child from Mexico

City to Nashville, from Buenos Aires to New York, spreading the good word."

"What is the good word?" I said.

"Here—" He slid the coffin from his lap to mine.

The weight was nothing. The Holy Infant gaped up at me.

"As you can see, Józef, the child is not yours. Not specifically. It is the same stuff as the Lord God, but born of our Klara—" Ligvogler went on talking.

I listened, watching the child. Its huge eyes, sunken blue globes, caused me to tremble. Tears fell from me to the child's silk dress. I heard the story of its birth and death.

Klara gave birth outside of Guaymas, Mexico, a port town, Ligvogler said.

In labor, she had walked through the dawn along the beach away from the town until she reached a great stone, he said.

Atop the stone at midday, she gave birth and slept, he said.

At night, wolves, seven or so, surrounded her on the stone.

When day broke, she flung the Holy Infant into the sea.

Ligvogler said that he swam through the surf and retrieved the infant.

The infant was dead.

The wolves swam in the waves, as well, he said.

Ligvogler carried the infant back to the top of the stone, but Klara was gone.

I went elsewhere. I remained on the bench in the Cunard with a child in a coffin on my lap, seated beside a madman, but I went elsewhere. I went into the darkness sealed within the infant's eyes. In that darkness I was naked, younger and whole. I had my left arm.

Klara was beside me, naked as well, though we could not turn to each other. A force held us frozen in the night sky, compelling our eyes to the sea. The Meteorite fought forward on the black water. A voice in our heads told us, "It will all be destroyed."

THOMAS FOX PARRY lives in
Philadelphia. *The Holy Infant* is
his first novel.